69

SIXTY-NINE

RYU MURAKAMI

Translated by
Ralph F. McCarthy

KODANSHA INTERNATIONAL
Tokyo • New York • London

For my friends back then

First published in Japanese in 1987 by Shueisha.

Distributed in the United States by Kodansha America, Inc., 114 Fifth Avenue, New York, N.Y. 10011, and in the United Kingdom and continental Europe by Kodansha Europe Ltd., Gillingham House, 38-44 Gillingham Street, London SW1V 1HU. Published by Kodansha International Ltd., 17-14 Otowa 1-chome, Bunkyo-ku, Tokyo 112, and Kodansha America, Inc. Copyright © 1993 by Kodansha International Ltd. All rights reserved. Printed in Japan.

Library of Congress CIP data available.

ISBN 4-7700-1736-7
First edition, 1993
93 94 95 10 9 8 7 6 5 4 3 2 1

CONTENTS

ARTHUR RIMBAUD

Nineteen sixty-nine was the year student uprisings shut down Tokyo University. The Beatles put out *The White Album*, *Yellow Submarine*, and *Abbey Road*, the Rolling Stones released their greatest single, "Honky Tonk Women," and people known as hippies wore their hair long and called for love and peace. In Paris, De Gaulle resigned. The war in Vietnam continued. High school girls used sanitary napkins, not tampons.

That's the sort of year 1969 was, when I began my third and final year of high school. I went to a college-prep high in a small city with an American military base on the western edge of Kyushu. Because I was in the science course, there were only seven girls in our class. Seven was better than none, as had been the case in my first two years, but most girls who take science are dogs, and I'm sorry to say that five of our seven were exactly that. One of the remaining pair, a girl with a face like a kewpie doll, was interested in nothing but math formulas and English vocabulary lists. Kewpie's father ran a lumberyard, and we figured you'd probably need a chisel to get inside her.

The other one happened to have the same name as the leader of the Japanese Red Army who was to shock the world three years later. Unlike her namesake, though, our Hiroko Nagata didn't suffer from an exophthalmic goiter.

There was a guy in our class who'd been lucky enough to take electric organ lessons with Hiroko when they were both in kindergarten. He was an honor student who hoped to go on to medical school at a national university, and so handsome that even girls from other high schools in the area knew about him. Unfortunately, however, he wasn't "wickedly" handsome but handsome in a fuzzy, unpolished sort of way, which I attributed to his having grown up in the country. If the rest of us spoke a dialect, Tadashi Yamada used an even rougher form of speech, a kind of *ultra*-dialect heard only in the coal-mining areas of Kyushu. Too bad. If Yamada had attended a junior high in the city he might have played the guitar, ridden a motorbike, known a lot about rock, been hip enough to order iced coffee instead of a plate of curry in coffee shops, and used marijuana, which was secretly all the rage at the time, as bait to hit up "bad" girls for a piece of ass.

But, though he lacked these refinements, he was still good-looking. We called him "Adama" in those days, because he reminded us a bit of the French singer Adamo.

My name is Kensuke Yazaki. People called me Kensuke, or Ken-san, or Ken-chan, or Ken-yan, or Ken-bo, or Ken-ken, but I asked my friends just to call me Ken. This was because I was a fan of the comic-book serial **"Ken the Wolfboy."**

It was spring of 1969.

The first exams of the year had finished that day. I'd

done miserably on all of them.

My grades had been dropping at a steady and alarming rate ever since I'd entered high school. There were various things one could blame for this—my parents' divorce, my younger brother's sudden suicide, the effect that reading Nietzsche had had on me, and the shock of learning that my grandmother had come down with an incurable disease—but none of them were true. The simple fact was that I hated studying.

It's also a fact, however, that in 1969 there was a convenient tendency to describe people who studied for college entrance exams as **capitalist lackeys**. Zenkyoto, the Joint Campus Action movement, had already begun to run out of steam, but it had at least managed to keep Tokyo University from functioning for a while.

Naively, we all hoped that something might actually change. And, according to the mood of the times, going to university wouldn't help you cope with that change, but smoking marijuana would.

Adama sat in the seat behind me. Each time we were told to pass our answer sheets to the front, I'd glance at his paper. He'd always answered about three times as many questions as I had.

When all the exams were over, I decided to skip out on homeroom and clean-up. I was hoping Adama would come with me.

"Hey, Adama. You know Cream?"

"Cream? Like ice cream?"

"No, you idiot. It's the name of a British rock group."

"Never heard of 'em."

"Boy, are you out of it. You're a lost cause, man."

"Me? Why?"

"Okay, then, you know who Rimbaud is?"

"What, another group?"

"He's a poet, dummy. Look. Read this, right here."

I showed him a book of **Rimbaud's poetry**. Too bad he didn't say "No thanks" and turn away. He went ahead and read it. Out loud. Looking back on that moment now, I can see that it was a major turning point in Adama's life.

> *I have found it*
> *What?*
> *Eternity*
> *The fusion of sun and sea*

Thirty minutes later we were standing in front of the gibbons' cage at the Nature Park, a long way from school and the whole routine that followed the exams, including lunch, and we were hungry. The mining town Adama grew up in was too far to commute from, so he stayed in a boarding-house in the city, and the people who ran the place packed a lunch for him every day. But I didn't bring a lunch; my mother always gave me a hundred and fifty yen to buy something with. If that figure surprises you, blame it on the inflation of the past fifteen years. In 1969 a hundred and fifty yen was big money. Kids from families poorer than mine managed to hold off starvation with just fifty yen a day—twenty for milk, ten for a sweet roll, and twenty for a curried bun.

With a hundred and fifty yen I could have had a bowl of noodles, milk, a curried bun, a melon roll, and a jelly doughnut. But I always made do with one bun—no milk—and saved the rest of my money to spend on books by Sartre, Genet, Céline, Camus, Bataille, Anatole France, and Kenzaburo Oe. In a pig's ass. What I really needed the cash for was to go to coffee shops and discos where I could hit up on loose chicks from Junwa Girls' High, a school with a **fox ratio** of over twenty percent.

Our city had two prefectural college-prep high schools, Northern High and Southern High; a prefectural industrial arts high school; a municipal commercial high school; three private girls' high schools; and a private coed high school. In small cities like ours, only the real duds went to private coed highs.

My own school, Northern High, was known for getting the best **college entrance** results; Southern High came second; the industrial arts school had a good baseball team; the commercial school was crawling with porkers; and Junwa, a private Catholic school where uniforms were optional, had, for some reason, a high ratio of foxes. Everyone knew that it had once been popular among the girls of Yamate, another private girls' high, to masturbate with radio tubes, and that many of the tubes had exploded, leaving them scarred for life; the girls of Koka High were so grim and gloomy that they rarely even rated as a topic of conversation; and it was said that when the kids at the private coed high, Asahi, shook their heads, you could hear a dry, rustling sound.

Status for a male student at Northern High consisted in having a member of the English Drama Club for a lady friend, having a Junwa girl of the uniformed sort for a lover and one of the streetclothes set for a mistress, having persuaded a student at Yamate to show you her scars, and having girls from Koka and Asahi supply you with spending money. Needless to say, however, life is never that accommodating, and, status aside, the more urgent problem was to find, as soon as possible, someone who would let you get into her pants. Which was why, in spite of having the princely sum of a hundred and fifty yen in my pocket, I had to make do with a single curried bun.

"Hey, man, I think I'll go get something to eat." We were still standing in front of the gibbons' cage, and my eyes were glued to Adama's box lunch as I said this.

"I'll split my lunch with you. Let's eat together."

Adama opened the little box, put half of its meager contents on the lid, and handed it to me. Adama had paid the bus fare from school to the Nature Park for both of us, and if it weren't for me he'd have been in homeroom at that very moment washing windows, serious lad that he was. It would have troubled my conscience if, on top of this, he were to give up half his lunch for my sake, so I politely declined. Like hell. I took my share and scarfed it down in three minutes flat, wondering all the while why he'd only given me one of his three fish-paste rolls, feeling disgust at his stinginess, and angrily reflecting that he had a better future in moneylending than in medicine.

Like a couple out on a picnic on their first date, once we'd eaten we had nothing to do. Gibbons can get on your nerves when you're bored. If our stomachs had been full, we could at least have taken a nap, but on half a lousy boardinghouse box lunch, forget it.

Not really having any choice, we started shooting the breeze.

"Ken-yan, what college you gonna go to?"

"Don't call me 'Ken-yan,' all right? Just Ken. I don't like it when people call me 'Ken-yan.'"

"Okay. You're going into medicine, right? You've been saying that ever since we were sophomores, haven't you?"

I was famous in my school for four things. The first was that in the fall of my sophomore year, I'd placed 321st out of some twenty thousand participants in a nationwide exam for people hoping to go on to medical school. The second was that I was a drummer in a band whose repertoire included songs by the Beatles, the Rolling Stones, the Walker Brothers, Procol Harum, the Monkees, and Paul Revere and the Raiders. The third was that I was in the newspaper club, and three times I'd put out editions without submitting them to the faculty advisor in advance, which resulted in their being **banned and confiscated**. The fourth was that in the third term of my sophomore year, I'd tried to put on a play for the "Goodbye, Seniors" party about a radical student group's campaign against a visit by an American aircraft carrier loaded with atomic missiles, and the play had been suppressed by the teachers. People thought I was peculiar.

"No, I'm not going into medicine. I'd never be accepted, anyway."

"What, then? Literature, I guess, huh?"

"Hell, no."

"No? So why do you read poetry and stuff?"

I couldn't tell him it was to help me seduce women.

13

Adama was a Hardboy at heart. Hardboys didn't approve of sucking up to women.

"I don't really like poetry. But Rimbaud's different. Everybody knows Rimbaud, man."

"They do?"

"Rimbaud was a big influence on Godard. You didn't know that?"

"Ah, Godard. I know who he is. I learned about him in World History."

"World History?"

"He was a poet from India, right?"

"That's Tagore, dummy. Godard's a film director."

I gave him a good ten-minute lecture on Godard. About how, being in the vanguard of the *nouvelle vague*, he was making one breakthrough film after another, about how spectacular the last scene in *Breathless* was, about the meaningless deaths in *Masculine–Feminine*, and about the subversive editing techniques in *Weekend*. Needless to say, I'd never seen a single film by the man. Godard didn't make it to small cities on the western edge of Kyushu.

"Literature, novels—if you ask me, stuff like that is finished, dead."

"So now it's movies, huh?"

"No, movies are finished, too."

"Well, what, then?"

"**Festivals**. Where you have theater and music and film all at the same time. You know what I mean?"

"No."

Yes, that's what I wanted to do—to set up a festival. *Fesutibaru*. The very word was exciting. There'd be every type of entertainment imaginable. We'd have plays and movies and live rock music, and all sorts of people would come. Girls from Junwa would come in droves. I'd play the drums, show a film I'd directed, and have the leading role in a play I'd written. Junwa would be there, the Northern High English Drama Club would be there, the radio tubes would be there, the rustle-heads would be there, and the gloomy girls from Koka would be there, crowding around to shower me with flowers and money.

"I've decided to organize a festival in this town," I said. "Adama, I'd like you to help me."

The rebel element at Northern High was divided into three main factions: the Greasers, the Rockers, and the Politicos. The Greasers were basically into drinking and smoking and chasing pussy, but occasionally indulged in fighting and gambling, and they had connections with the local yakuza. The central figure in this group was a guy named Yuji Shirokushi. The Rockers—also known as the Artistes —carried copies of *New Music* magazine, Jimi Hendrix's *Smash Hits*, and *Art Today*, grew their hair as long as possible, and walked around flashing the V-sign and mumbling "Peace." The Politicos were aligned with the Students and Workers Liberation Front at Nagasaki University, and had pooled their money to rent a room in town to use as a hideout. They plastered the walls of the room with posters of Chairman Mao and Che Guevara and surreptitiously circulated leaflets at school. At the core of this faction were two guys named Goro Narushima and Ryo Otaki. There were other groups, too—the Rightists, who were fans of some rabid old prewar imperialist; the Folkies, who were into folk music; the Literati, who put out their own little magazine; the Bikers, and so on—but none of them had many members or were capable of mobilizing large numbers of people.

Although I didn't belong to any of these factions, I was on good terms with members of all the three main ones. Being a drummer, I often sat in on jam sessions with the Rockers, and I sometimes drank beer with Shirokushi and his gang and showed up for debates at Narushima and Otaki's hideout.

I also had a friend in the newspaper club named Iwase whose family ran a sewing goods shop and who was exactly what you'd expect someone whose family ran a sewing goods shop to be like. We'd been in the same class in our first year in high school. He was a puny little guy, and a bit dim-witted, but he was hooked on anything to do with Art. Maybe it was connected with the fact that his father had died and he'd grown up with four older sisters, but he'd been keen to make friends with me because my father was an artist. Anyway, Iwase shared my dream of setting up a festival. We were both avid readers of *Art Today* and *New Music*, and had been blown away by the rock fests and happenings described in these magazines. What rock fests and happenings had in common, and what appealed to us about them, were naked women. Neither of us said as much in so many words, but we were obviously of one mind on that score.

"Ken-san," Iwase had said to me one day, "let's make friends with Yamada. He's a good-looking guy, and he gets good grades. With you and him working together, we can do anything."

I asked him if he was trying to say I wasn't good-looking

and didn't get good grades, and he said no three times:

"No, no, no. It's like, Ken-san, you're, how should I put this, it's like, don't get me wrong, your ideas or whatever, the things you think up, are great, but, well, you never really do anything, right? I mean, I don't mean you never do anything, but it's like, girls, food, whatever's right in front of you, right?"

In our second year, Iwase and I had decided we wanted to make films and started saving money to buy an eight-millimeter camera. We pooled our allowances and lunch money, but when we'd saved up six hundred yen, I'd gone and treated a Junwa girl to a lunch of chicken and rice, with cream puffs for dessert. That's the sort of thing he meant.

He was right, though. Adama was good-looking and did well in school, and as a result had quite a following. He'd also been on the basketball team until his junior year and earned a reputation for helping solve a lot of his teammates' personal, woman, and money problems. In order to make our festival a reality, we had to get him to join forces with us.

Adama and I left the gibbons' cage and climbed the observation tower. The sun had begun to dip toward the sea.

"I guess everybody's cleaning the classroom right now, eh?" he said, gazing out at the bay and smiling. I smiled, too. Adama was learning the joy of ditching class. He asked me to show him the book of poems again.

> *I have found it*
> *What?*
> *Eternity*
> *The fusion of sun and sea*

Adama read it aloud. Peering at the ribbon of sunlight sparkling on the water, he asked me if he could borrow the book. I lent it to him, as well as an album by **Cream** and another by Vanilla Fudge.

That's how 1969, the third most interesting of my thirty-two years, began.

We were seventeen.

IRON BUTTERFLY

In 1969 we were seventeen. And we still had our **cherries**. To be a virgin at that age is nothing to be particularly proud of and nothing to be particularly ashamed of, but it's something that weighs on your mind.

The winter I turned sixteen I'd run away from home. My reason for doing so was that I'd perceived a fundamental contradiction in the entire entrance examination system and wanted to get away from my home and school and out on the streets in order to better think about this and to ponder the significance of the struggle that had developed that year between the student radicals and the aircraft carrier *Enterprise*. Sorry. That's not exactly true. The truth is that I didn't want to take part in a long-distance race at school. Long-distance running had always been a weak point with me. I'd hated it ever since junior high school. Now that I'm thirty-two and wiser, of course, I still hate it.

It wasn't that I was a wimp or anything; it's just that I had a habit of abruptly slowing down to a walk and deciding that I'd run enough. It wasn't that I'd get a pain in my side, or feel sick or dizzy, either; just that as soon as I felt a bit tired I started walking. If anything, in fact, I was healthier

19

than most. My lung capacity measured over 6,000 cc, and soon after I got to high school I'd found myself among thirteen or fourteen boys summoned to the track and field clubroom. The coach was a young guy, a recent graduate of the Nippon College of Health and Physical Education. He was one of six new P.E. instructors the school had hired to help prepare us for the National Athletic Meet, which was to be held in Nagasaki two years later. One was an expert at judo, one at team handball, one at basketball, one at field events, one at swimming, and one at long-distance running. In 1969, when "Smash the National Athletic Meet" became one of the rallying cries of our student uprising, these experts were a convenient target to attack. They didn't like us much, either.

Kawasaki, the running coach, had a square head, curly hair, and short but powerful legs that had earned him Japan's third-best time in the 5,000 meters. This was the spiel he made us listen to in the clubroom:

"For fifteen-year-olds, you boys have all got terrific lungs. I want you to form a long-distance relay team. No one's forcing you to join, of course, but I strongly recommend that you do. You may not know it, but you were all born to be long-distance runners, and we're going to make champions out of you."

I was appalled to learn that my cardio-pulmonary system had condemned me from birth to this dismal prospect.

Once winter vacation was over, all our P.E. classes were devoted to training us for the annual school marathon. That first year, I was subjected to a constant stream of abuse from Kawasaki. Because I tended to slow abruptly to a walk, he called me—I quote—"a scumbag."

"Listen," he said. "Running is the basis of all sports. No, it's more than that—it's the basis of life. People are always comparing life to a marathon, right? Yazaki, you bum, you've got a lung capacity of 6,100, and you just slack off and haven't run the distance once. You're a scumbag. You'll end up in the gutter, wait and see."

"Scumbag," "bum"—is that any way for an instructor to speak to an impressionable teenager? Not that I couldn't understand where he was coming from. It was true, after all, that having run for about five hundred meters, I'd stop to stroll along with all the slobs, chatting about the Beatles and girls and motorbikes and what have you, and then, when there were five hundred meters or so left to go, I'd start running again and wouldn't even be breathing hard as I crossed the finish line.

"It's all my fault. I didn't bring you up properly," my long-suffering mother, who was in Korea during the war, says even to this day. When things get a bit difficult, I quit; when some little thing stands in my way, I just give up and go with the flow; always looking for the easy way out, the path of least resistance—that's me, she says. I hate to say it, but she's right.

Nevertheless, I did take part in the long-distance race my first year. The course covered seven kilometers: from the school to Mt. Eboshi, halfway up the mountain, and back. Along with the geeks, the physically unfit, and my fellow gutless wonders, I walked silently up the mountain road to the turning point, being passed by a number of girls who'd started five minutes later, then bounded lightly back down the road to the school, where most of the students were already wrapped in blankets, gasping for breath, or being led off, puking, to the first-aid room, or drinking hot glucose with trembling hands; and when I crossed the finish line, number 598 out of 662 male students, whistling "A Day in the Life," not only Kawasaki but most of the teachers there agreed that I was scum.

Being the **sensitive child** I was, I didn't want to go through that sort of thing again, so in the winter of my second year, when I was sixteen, I ran away from home.

I withdrew the nearly thirty thousand yen I had in postal savings and headed for the sprawling metropolis of Hakata. In addition to avoiding the school marathon, there was one other thing I wanted to accomplish during this trip.

Losing my virginity.

As soon as I reached Hakata, I checked into the ANA Hotel—the fanciest hotel in all of Kyushu at the time—then put on my George Harrison–style tweed jacket and hit the streets. I was strolling down an avenue lined with leafless trees, singing "She's a Rainbow," when a woman's voice said, "Hi there." It was dusk, and the sky was a pale, heart-stirring purple. The voice belonged to a woman several years older than me who looked a lot like Marianne Faithfull and was driving a silver E-type Jaguar. She beckoned to me with her forefinger, opened the door of the Jag, and said, "I have a favor to ask you. Would you mind getting in? Please?" I got in. Her perfume was intoxicating. "You see," she said, "I used to be a top fashion model but I got into a bit of trouble in Tokyo and had to hide out down here for a while and now I'm working at a very exclusive club called Cactus and I got involved with this customer and it's turning into a problem, you see, because he's a yakuza who owns a lumberyard and he wants to set me up as his mistress and won't take no for an answer but, well, I don't really need the money and I don't want to be anybody's mistress so I told him I've got a younger brother who's my only living relative and he's got heart disease so I have to stay with him, but I don't actually have any brothers so I was planning to get somebody to play the part but I never got around to it and today's the day I'm supposed to go talk to the guy, so…" She asked me if I'd be willing to pretend to be her brother for just one day. I looked at her silver fox coat and her crimson nail polish and her miniskirt and her long, slender legs and naturally agreed to help. She took me to a riverfront building, where the yakuza had an office on the seventh floor. He was a huge guy in his early sixties with a bull neck and seven young punks working for him. Some of the punks had tattoos. The guy said, "He looks awful healthy for a kid with heart disease." Then he slapped himself on the chest and said, "Anyway, just leave it to me. I'll pay for the operation." "We don't need your money," I said. "My sister's not going to be your mistress, and that's all there is to it." His sidekicks got pissed off at this and started shouting, and two of them pulled knives out of their belts. I stood in front of the woman to protect her and said, "If you've got to kill somebody, kill me." Then I made up some stuff about how our parents had divorced and we'd been raised by our grandmother and she'd died four years ago and now it was just me and my sister and we'd promised each other to stick together through thick and thin and that someday we'd find a way to be happy no matter what. Deep down inside, as it turned out, the yakuza was a real softie, and by the time I'd finished he had tears in his eyes and was mumbling, "Okay, you win." The woman was thrilled. To celebrate, we had a full-course dinner at a French restaurant, where she poured me some red wine and whispered, "You're quite a guy, aren't you?" Afterward, she took me to her place. It was a big open-style condominium, the kind you see in the movies, with a king-size bed right in the middle of it. The woman giggled and said, "I'm going to take a shower. Don't go away!" and disappeared into the bathroom. I kept telling myself, *Keep cool, keep cool*, but I didn't know what the hell to do and just sat there pulling the zipper on my pants up and down. Eventually she reappeared wearing a see-through black negligee and said, "You don't know how grateful I am. Tonight I'm all yours.... I know that's not enough, though ... so I want you to have the Jag as well.... It suits you perfectly...."

At least, that's the story I made up for my friends when I got back. The truth is a little different.

The first thing I did when I reached Hakata was take in a triple bill of porno films. Then, after a bowl of noodles and some fried pork dumplings, I went to a strip show in one of those hole-in-the-wall sort of joints. It was past 1:00 A.M. when I left there, and as I was strolling along beside the river, an elderly pimp—a woman—approached me and said, "Like to get your pipes cleaned, son?" I gave the old crone three thousand yen, and she took me to a grimy little inn where a woman with dark rings around her eyes, like a raccoon, called out "Good *eeeve*ning." Looking at the raccoon's round belly, I thought of my mother, who right at that moment was probably in tears, worrying about me. I began to feel like crying myself, and suddenly losing my virginity didn't seem so important, but I let the raccoon help me off with my clothes. She was obviously in a hurry to get it over with, but I just couldn't get it up. "It's no use," she said finally. "I'll spread my legs and let you look. You can do yourself." It was the first time I'd ever seen what she showed me. It wasn't that big a deal—not as big as the ten thousand yen she took off me when I told her to pack it in. I left the place in a mood of black despair and continued walking along the river. Half my money was gone, so I decided to sleep in the waiting room at the station rather than stay at a cheap hotel. I asked a salaryman type in a suit and tie which way the station was. When I told him I was planning to sleep there, he offered to let me stay at his apartment. I was pretty miserable, and it was nice to be shown some kindness, so I went with him. Once we got there, he made me a corned beef sandwich, which I appreciated, but, as anyone might have guessed, this led suddenly to a hand on my crotch and him trying to kiss me on the lips, whispering "You don't mind, do you?" It was getting to be just one damn thing after another, and I'd had enough. I reached into my bag, pulled out a camping knife, and stuck it in the table. The guy started trembling all over. It occurred to me then that I might be able to recoup the thirteen thousand yen I'd given the old woman and the raccoon, plus four thousand for a hotel room, but—why did nothing seem to go right?—I suddenly had to piss. **Hey! Where's the toilet?"** I shouted. It's hard to imagine a more ludicrous line for someone wielding a knife. No sooner had I stepped inside the bathroom than I heard the man run out the door. As I was pissing I began to realize that what I'd done might be construed as armed robbery, and I convinced myself that he'd be back shortly with the cops. I had to escape. It's at times like this, though, that a piss lasts forever. When I finally finished I was out of the fag's apartment in seconds flat. I can't tell you how ridiculous I felt, sprinting down the streets of Hakata after I'd run away from home to avoid a footrace. I ran much harder than I ever had in any P.E. class, and it was dawn before I stopped. I staggered into a fairly large park and guzzled water from a drinking fountain, then lay down on a bench to wait for the sun to rise. I figured I'd probably feel better once I'd warmed up a bit. I fell asleep for a while as I was waiting, and awoke to the soft touch of sunlight on my cheek and a loud twanging in my ears. Through the white morning mist that hung over the park I could see a small stage where a bunch of dudes with long hair were tuning some instruments. There were no drums on the stage, and the guitars were acoustic ones with mikes attached, so I figured they were folkies. In those days folk-singers were on the increase even in Kyushu, thanks to the media coverage of the hootenannies held on the plaza outside Shinjuku Station in Tokyo. People gradually began to gather. It was folk music, all right. They started playing by the time the mist cleared. A guy with hair down to his shoulders, a beard, and a dirty jumper sang stuff by various boring protest singers. A banner on the stage said "Presented by the Fukuoka Chapter of the Peace for Vietnam Committee." I hated folk. I didn't like the Peace for Vietnam Committee, either. Living in a town with an American military base made you realize just how rich and powerful America was. A high school student who heard the roar of Phantom jets every day didn't have to be a genius to know that singing folk songs made about as much difference as farting. People started clapping their hands in time, and I looked on from a distance, muttering *You idiots*. They made speeches between songs: the usual crap—"U.S. out of Vietnam!" and so on. There'd been a girl in my junior high school named Chiyoko Masuda who became a navy whore. She was in the calligraphy club and used to win a lot of prizes. A serious sort. In my second year there, she sent me a love letter, saying she wanted to correspond with me. She said she liked Hesse, and that it had made her happy to hear me mention during a class meeting that I liked Hesse, too, and that it would be nice if we could write each other letters about Hesse and things. I had a crush on a different girl and never wrote back. Then one day during my first year of high school I saw Chiyoko Masuda, her hair dyed red and her face caked with makeup, walking arm in arm with a black sailor. Our eyes met, but she ignored me. There were some navy groupies who lived in a house near mine, and I'd peeked through their windows a few times when they were having sex with American servicemen. I wondered if Chiyoko, too, sucked black guys' dicks. I couldn't figure out how calligraphy and Hesse led to black dick. Listening to the pious shit the Peace for Vietnam Committee was belting out, I began to get depressed again and thought of moving on, but I was tired and, besides, I didn't have anywhere to go. As I sat there grumbling to myself about how dumb the folkies were, I noticed a girl standing next to me, inhaling paint thinner fumes from a plastic bag. "You don't like folk?" said **the thinner girl**. "No, I don't," I said. "My name's Ai-chan," she told me. She had a slightly moronic face. We talked about Iron Butterfly and the Dynamites and Procol Harum. Ai-chan's eyes were bleary. She took my hand and pulled me to my feet, and we started walking away. Ai-chan

27

had been a beautician whose dream was to go to America and see the Grateful Dead, but as the paychecks came in she began to realize that she'd never be able to save enough for the trip, so she became a street kid instead. We had a cream soda, went to a rock café and listened to the Doors, hung around in a department store and ate a bowl of noodles and tempura to kill time till evening, then went to a disco, where they turned us away saying street kids weren't allowed inside. Ai-chan invited me to her house and said she'd let me do it to her. It seemed to me that a rock-loving, thinner-sniffing, slightly backward chick was the ideal person to offer my virginity to. If I got into the pants of one of the fair ladies of the English Drama Club, say, she might start talking marriage; the raccoon, on the other hand, would have been a real downer. Ai-chan's place was on a hill on the outskirts of town. It was actually a *house*, which seemed suspicious, and, sure enough, her mother came to the door. With tears in her eyes, she started screeching about high school and dropping out and making a living and Papa's company and the neighbors and suicide and so on. Ai-chan, loaded on thinner fumes, ignored her and tried to drag me inside, but I hung back when a huge man materialized in the doorway and glared at me. The man snatched the plastic bag out of Ai-chan's hand and slapped her. Then he turned to me and shouted, "Get out of here!" I followed his advice. As I was leaving, Ai-chan took my hand and said, "Sorry."

I'd had enough of Hakata by then, so I went to Kagoshima, then took a boat to Amami-Oshima Island. I was still a virgin. What made it worse was that when I returned to school after a couple of weeks, I learned that the long-distance race had been postponed because of rain.

So now, at seventeen, I was still as pure as the driven snow. I knew one seventeen-year-old, however, who was getting laid left and right. His name was Kiyoshi Fukushima, and he was the bassist in Coelacanth, the band I played drums in. We called him Fuku-chan. Though only a teen-ager, Fuku-chan had the face of a middle-aged man. He was a big guy, too.

Both of us had been on the rugby team for part of our first year. The rugby clubroom was right next to the one for the track and field people. There was a second-year student, a sprinter who'd made a name for himself by setting the pre-fectural record in the hundred meters, and Fuku-chan and I bumped into him outside the clubroom one day. Even then Fuku-chan looked as if he were twenty-something, and the runner assumed he was an upperclassman and bowed and rapped out a hearty greeting. Fuku-chan thought this was amusing, so he played the part, saying, "Well, how's it going, squirt? You getting any faster?" "Yes, sir," said the run-ner, standing stiffly at attention. "I'm down to 10.4 in the hundred." "Oh, yeah? Well, keep working at it. You'll im-prove." We both had a good laugh about this, but later, when the runner found out that he'd been taken for a ride, he and the other upperclassmen on the track and rugby teams beat the shit out of Fuku-chan.

Good old Fuku-chan. Whenever I asked him how one went about getting chicks the way he did, he always told me the same thing: **Don't aim too high**.

The first thing I wanted to do to get our festival going

was to make a film, and no sooner had Adama joined forces with us than he amazed me by getting his hands on an eight-millimeter Bell & Howell. He'd gone around asking all the younger kids if any of them had a movie camera, and when one said yes, he'd had Yuji Shirokushi, the head Greaser, threaten the guy till he handed it over.

The next order of business was to find a leading lady. I insisted it had to be Kazuko Matsui. Adama and Iwase both said I was dreaming. After all, Kazuko "Lady Jane" Matsui was such a stone fox that she was famous even in other schools in the city, and, what's more, she was a member of the hallowed English Drama Club.

LADY JANE

Making films had been the hip thing to do ever since a Tokyo high school student beat all the veteran independent avant-garde directors to take a Grand Prix at the Film Biennale. Everyone agreed that film-making was the most advanced of the arts, and that it was **easy**, too. It's funny: not one of us—Iwase, Adama, or me—had ever seen a single underground movie, yet we all dreamed of making one. It was like the French living on the Atlantic coast under the Nazi occupation, dreaming of an Allied landing.

"Okay, here's how we'll go about it. You listening? Never mind the Godard method—improvisation and all that. We'll write a script. We'll make it, you know, how should I put this, sort of, like, muddy, you know, Kenneth Anger style. And the camerawork we'll do like Jonas Mekas."

Adama and Iwase nodded and grunted their agreement as I rattled on, but the truth is that none of us had any idea what sort of film to make. All we knew was that we wanted to make one, like girls whose only ambition is to fall in love.

On a beautiful afternoon in late April, Iwase, Adama, and I, our hearts all aflutter, went to watch the English Drama

Club rehearse. Those lovely young ladies, the pride of Northern High, were cooking up something by Shakespeare in the hope of winning first prize in the All-Kyushu English Drama Competition. The entrance to the auditorium was already overflowing with male students. Most of them were of the Greaser faction, and in the middle of the crowd stood Yuji Shirokushi in bell-bottom pants, snakeskin sandals, and a school uniform jacket with the collar unfastened. Shirokushi had been in love with Kazuko Matsui since our first year in high school. Why is it that the greasy hoodlum types always fall for the classiest women? It goes without saying that the object of his affection wouldn't have been seen dead with him.

Shirokushi saw us and waved. "Ken-yan. What are you doing here?"

"Just, you know, thought I'd brush up on my English a bit."

Shirokushi peered at my face and said, "Bullshit."

Why is it that the greasy hoodlum types can always tell when a regular guy is lying?

"Who'd you come to see? Yumi? Masako? Mieko? Sakiko?"

Yes, there were any number of famous beauties in the English Drama Club. Iwase, Adama, and I exchanged glances, and suddenly Shirokushi seemed to get the picture.

"Don't tell me… Not my little Kazuko? Eh? You came to see Kazuko?"

"Well, yeah, but it's not what you think."

The words were hardly out of my mouth when he whipped a knife out of his pocket and stuck it in my thigh. No, but he did grab me by the collar.

"Not even you can hit up on Kazuko and get away with

it, Ken-yan," he said menacingly, but when Adama told him to cut it out he immediately released me, smiled, and said, "Just kidding, just kidding." Adama explained things to him.

"Yuji, you don't understand, man. Ken wants to make a movie. You know the eight-millimeter camera we got off that kid? Ken's gonna make a movie with it."

"A movie? So what? What's that got to do with Kazuko?"

"Well, you see, it's just that we were hoping she'd agree to be the leading lady," I said, trying to sound as **suave** as possible.

"Yuji, it'll be the first time a student at Northern High ever made a movie. Who else could be the star, man? Huh? If we don't get Kazuko Matsui to be the star, who we gonna get?"

Leave it to Adama to think of exactly the right thing to say. Shirokushi's entire face lit up. "Yeah. Yeah, you're right. Who else could it be but Kazuko?"

"See what I mean? So if we don't let Ken have a good look at her, how's he gonna come up with the right image?"

Shirokushi nodded several times as Adama spoke, then took my hand and shook it, saying, "Yeah, that makes sense. But listen, man, you better make her look good. Better than Brigitte Bardot, even." He moved up to the front of the crowd, kicking people in the butt to clear a space for us. The idea of making Kazuko Matsui the star of our film had excited him, and now he was rattling on about how we should use something by Yujiro Ishihara for the theme song, and how about if Kazuko played a bus guide who was raised in an orphanage, and he himself would be a hit man, see, and …

"Ken," Adama whispered to me, "this is not cool. If

Kazuko Matsui sees this she won't want to be in the film."
He had a point. If Lady Jane saw us here with Shirokushi
babbling "movie movie movie movie," she'd freeze us out
completely. She hated the guy. Adama didn't miss a trick.

"Ken, why don't you go check it out for yourself. She's
probably in the room backstage right now."

"What are you talking about? It's all chicks back there."

"You're in the newspaper club, right?"

"Yeah?"

"Well, all you have to do is say you're getting material
together for an article."

So I ended up going on my own to that holy sanctuary,
the room that housed the English Drama Club. When I
looked back over my shoulder, everyone in the auditorium
was cheering me on. Some even waved their caps and
shouted, "Go get 'em, Ken!" Adama, in the meantime, was
trying to smooth things over with Shirokushi, who wanted
to go with me.

The room smelled like a meadow full of flowers. It made
you want to start singing **"Daisy Chain."** My only
problem was that I didn't know what to say. To start off with
something like "Er" or "Good afternoon" or "Excuse me"
would have been too ordinary, but I couldn't think of anything else. I was just toying with the idea of trying a bit of
English when the faculty advisor for the club, a guy named
Yoshioka, came striding out of the room toward me. He was
a middle-aged pain in the ass who plastered his hair down
with pomade and thought he was hot stuff because he
always wore an English suit.

"What is it?" he said in a tone of voice that made it clear

he meant, *How dare you set foot in this sacred place.*

"I'm, uh, in the newspaper club. My name's—"

"Yazaki. I know your name. I teach grammar to your class, for heaven's sake."

"Yes, sir."

"What do you mean, 'Yes, sir'? How would you know? You're almost never there."

Just my luck. I hadn't expected somebody like this to appear and start laying a rap on me. With him in particular, I was at a disadvantage. Yoshioka was a bastard, but since he was also too much of a gentleman ever to hit anyone, I made a habit of cutting his class. I'd flunked his first exam, too. He peered at me from behind his black-framed glasses.

"So? What do you want? Don't tell me you want to join the drama club. You haven't a hope."

A burst of gay laughter came from inside the room. The foxes were listening to our little dialogue. I couldn't afford to back down now.

"I'm here to research an article."

"About what?"

"The war in Vietnam."

"That's news to me. You know how it works: first you ask the advisor of the newspaper club for permission, then the advisor talks to me, and I give the okay. You can't just decide these things for yourself."

In Kyushu, like everywhere else, high school newspaper clubs tended to be dens of rebellion, and in our school no club was allowed to align itself with any other. The teachers' greatest fear was of the students getting organized. Even if members of the newspaper club wanted to do something as harmless as carrying out a survey or collecting information, we had to clear it with the faculty advisor first. Unofficial gatherings were absolutely forbidden. This system was endorsed by the student council. The school laid down the law and used the yes-men in the student council to make it look as if *we* had made the rules ourselves. It might as well have been a prison. A colony under military rule. It was sickening.

"All right, the truth is, I'm not really here to research an article."

"What, then?"

"I just, uh, came to have a little chat."

"Can't you see we're busy here? No one has time for that sort of thing."

Inside the room, the girls were cutting stencils to use for mimeographing the script. *Squeak, creak, creak, squeak.* Half of them were ignoring Yoshioka and me, and the others were watching us. Kazuko Matsui was watching. She held a stylus thoughtfully against her cheek. She had eyes like Bambi's. Eyes a man could fight and die for.

I sneered and said, "How ridiculous can you get?"

Yoshioka was taken aback. "What are you talking about?"

"Shakespeare—where's that at? Thousands of people are dying every day in Vietnam, and you're doing Shakespeare. It's ridiculous. Mr. Yoshioka …"

"What?"

"Look out the window at that harbor. Every day American battleships sail out of there to go and kill people."

He was flustered. Teachers this far out in the sticks didn't know how to handle students with anti-establishment ideas.

They couldn't just slap you around, the way they did the usual deadbeat types.

"I'm going to report this to the teacher in charge of your club."

"Do you *like* war, Mr. Yoshioka?"

"What sort of thing is that to say?"

Yoshioka had lived through World War II. He'd probably known his share of misery. His face clouded over. War was convenient. You could always use it in your arguments with teachers; it made them uncomfortable, particularly when they were obliged in class to say that war was bad. They'd always try to dodge the issue.

"Yazaki, get out of here. We're busy."

"Are you against war?"

I wondered if he'd served in the military. Being small, and an arty type, he would have been bullied like hell.

"If you're against it, it's cowardly not to speak out."

"What has that got to do with anything?"

"Plenty. American troops are using our harbor. To kill people."

"That's not for high school students to worry about."

"So who's supposed to worry about it?"

"Yazaki, deliver yourself of these opinions once you've graduated from college, got a job, married, and had children of your own. Once you're a full-fledged adult."

Dipshit. **"Deliver yourself,"** my ass.

"Oh. So you can't be opposed to war unless you're an adult? Does that mean children don't die in war? High school students don't die in war?"

Yoshioka's face turned beet red. Just then the running

coach, Kawasaki, passed by with the judo coach, Aihara. I didn't notice them. I was telling Yoshioka that not to do anything about something was the same as approving of it, and asking him if it was okay for a teacher to approve of killing people, when Aihara came up behind me, grabbed me by the hair, slapped me across the face three times, and threw me to the floor. "*Yazakiiiiii!*" he shouted. Aihara was a bonehead from some crummy right-wing college, but he was also a scary guy with cauliflower ears who'd once been the national middleweight judo champion. "On your *feeeet!*" he screamed. First he knocks me down, then he tells me to stand up. This pissed me off, but the cauliflower ears and squashed nose commanded a certain respect, so I rose groggily to my feet. "You little *turrrrd!* Who do you think you're talking *tooooo!*" He slapped me again. The palms of his hands were thick and hard, so even a slap packed quite a punch. "For somebody who can't even run a race you run off at the mouth just fine, don't you?" This was Kawasaki's contribution. Why did he have to bring up that race crap at a time like this? I could feel tears of vexation welling up in my eyes. If I cried, it was all over: Kazuko Matsui was watching. Aihara grinned. When you were a guy with a chip on your shoulder about graduating from some shit college, nothing in life gave more satisfaction than beating up kids like me. Yuji Shirokushi and his group got their share of grief from Aihara, too. During judo practice, he'd throw them down with a choke-hold, or crush their nuts, or hurl them against the wall, or grab them by the ear and kick their feet out from under them, stuff like that. You don't stand much of a chance against a teacher with muscles.

Grabbing me by the hair again, he proceeded to drag me

all the way down to the teachers' room. Shirokushi, Adama, and Iwase gaped at us as we went by. "Don't … don't tell me," the Greaser said. "Don't tell me he tried to jump Kazuko!"

They made me stand there in a corner for an hour. The worst part about it was that every time a teacher passed by he'd ask me what I'd done, and I'd have to explain it all over again. The man in charge of the newspaper club and the faculty advisor both had to apologize to Yoshioka, Kawasaki, and Aihara. Which meant that two teachers had to eat dirt because of me.

And I hadn't even had a chance to talk to Lady Jane.

"Masutabe-chan—that's quite a name you've got. Mind if we just call you 'Handjob'?"

Only Adama and I enjoyed the joke. Tatsuo Masutabe—the second-year student who'd "lent" us his eight-millimeter camera—was a serious little guy. He was also a member of the political group headed by Narushima and Otaki, and he'd come to tell us he wouldn't let us use the thing unless we were going to make a film with a radical theme. Adama tried to reassure him by saying that even if we didn't deal directly with the people's struggle, there were lots of ways to go about it, like, for example, Godard-type symbolism and so on, right? But Masutabe asked us to talk it over with his group.

"Good morning."

It was a voice like a spring breeze. I stopped on the hill in front of the school and turned around, and there stood my Bambi: Kazuko Matsui. A shiver ran through me.

"Oh, hi there," I said with a smile, putting my arm around her shoulders and stroking her hair. Fat chance. I could hardly even speak.

"Bus?" she said. She was asking how I got to school.

"No. On foot. You?"

"Bus."

"Bus crowded?"

"Yes. But not too bad."

"Oh. Um, you know, I was wondering ... Who started calling you 'Lady Jane'?"

"An upperclassman."

"From the Stones song?"

"Uh-huh. I used to like that song."

"It's a good one. You like the Stones?"

"I don't know that much about them, really. I like Dylan, the Beatles.... But my favorite is **Simon and Garfunkel**."

"Oh yeah? I like them, too."

"Have you got their records?"

"Sure. *Wednesday Morning 3 A.M.*, *Parsley, Sage, Rosemary & Thyme*, and, uh, *Homeward Bound*."

"What about *Bookends*?"

"Got it."

"Really? Could I borrow it?"

"Sure."

"Honest? Thanks! I love that song 'At the Zoo.' Don't you think the lyrics are great?"

"Oh, yeah—fantastic."

I was trying to think of a way to get my hands on *Bookends*. I'd have to buy it today, no matter what. I'd scrape up the money somehow, get Adama and Iwase to contribute. Surely they'd see the necessity. Anything for our leading lady.

"Are you always thinking about those things?"

"What things?"

"The things you were saying to Mr. Yoshioka the other day."

"Ah. Vietnam, and all that?"

"Yes."

"Well, not especially, but it's everywhere you look, right? In the news and stuff."

"Do you read a lot of books and things?"

"Sure."

"If there's anything interesting, would you lend it to me?"

I was wishing this hill in front of the school would never end. I wanted to go on talking to her for ever and ever. It was the first time I'd ever realized how wonderful just walking with a beautiful woman could make you feel.

"You know how on TV you see a lot of students demonstrating and barricading school buildings and everything? It's like a completely different world to me, but … but I feel like I understand them."

"Oh?"

"You said Shakespeare was ridiculous, didn't you? I think so, too."

"You do?"

"Simon and Garfunkel, people like that, you can really understand what they're talking about. Shakespeare's not like that, though."

We reached the school. I promised to lend her *Bookends*,

and we said bye-bye and went our separate ways. Even after we'd parted, I felt as if I were in a meadow full of flowers.

Adama was surprised when I suddenly suggested we **barricade the school**. I was somehow under the impression that Kazuko Matsui had said she was attracted to boys who got involved in barricades and demonstrations.

"Well, we promised Masutabe anyway," he said. "I guess it wouldn't hurt to go check out the Politicos' place one time."

DANIEL COHN-BENDIT

The Sasebo Northern High School Joint Campus Action Committee. This was the name of the organization headed by Otaki and Narushima, and their hangout was above Sasebo Station. When I say "above," I don't mean it was on the second floor of the station. Sasebo, like Nagasaki, is a town with a lot of hills. It's a perfect natural harbor, with mountains behind the town providing protection from the wind, and a low, curving coastline—a narrow strip of level ground packed with department stores and movie theaters and shopping streets and, of course, the American military base. The base occupies the very best land, as it does in every town that has one.

The headquarters of the Northern High JCA Committee was on the second floor of a cigarette shop at the top of a long, steep hill north of the station.

"Doesn't this hill ever end?" Adama said. Sweat was dripping down his face. About ninety-eight percent of the citizens of Sasebo lived up on these slopes. The children would scramble down the hills to play in town, then trudge back home, tired and hungry.

Like most cigarette shops, this one was equipped with an

old lady who you weren't quite sure was still alive.

"Good afternoon!" we called out cheerfully, but she didn't so much as twitch. I thought she was dead. Adama thought she might be a wax figure, a display of some sort. She wasn't asleep; she was sitting hunched over, with her hands folded on her lap, and her eyes were open. We were a bit worried about her and decided to wait and see if she blinked, but her eyelids were as droopy as eyelids can get, and we had to watch closely. Beneath the eaves was a bed of withered cosmos or something. The wind played through the old lady's thin hair. Just as we'd come to the conclusion that she really was a wax figure, or a mummy, her eyelids sagged shut and creaked open again. Adama and I smiled at each other.

At the side of the stairway next to the shop entrance was a sign that said "Northern High Economic Research Group" —if you can call a rain-smeared piece of drawing paper a sign. We climbed the stairs. It was dark in there. I asked Adama why the lighting in Japanese buildings was so bad, and he said it was because the Japanese were hopeless sex fiends. Maybe so.

Nobody was in the hangout. It was a twelve-mat room. Posters of Che Guevara, Mao Tse-tung, and **Trotsky** covered the sliding doors. There was a mimeograph machine on a desk and some serious-looking paperbacks, a cheap acoustic guitar, a bullhorn, and copies of the Students and Workers Liberation Front newsletter.

"Looks kind of obscene, doesn't it?" Adama said. He was eyeing the futon spread out on the floor, and the pillows and tissue paper scattered around it. It may have had something to do with the bad lighting in Japanese buildings, but there was always a seamy sort of feeling to these radical hangouts. If they had a futon, it meant that people spent the night here sometimes. The political faction included some high school girls—not girls from Northern High, apparently, but from the commercial high school. No combination could be more obscene than a futon, tissue paper, and girls from a commercial high school.

Iwase arrived about ten minutes later, dripping with sweat and carrying three cartons of coffee-flavored milk. As I drank mine I wished I had a roll to go with it. Iwase picked up the cheap guitar and started to play "Sometimes I Feel Like a Motherless Child." Ever since Elvis, guitars had been the one thing no kid in the nation wanted to be without. Those who couldn't afford one made do with ukeleles, which was the only reason there'd been a brief Hawaiian music craze. Electric guitars became the big thing when I was in junior high school. Tesco guitars, Guyatone amps, Pearl drums. Instruments by makers like Gibson and Fender and Music Man and Roland and Paiste existed only in magazines. Once the Ventures fad was over and the era of the Beatles and other vocal-oriented groups arrived, everybody wanted a semi-acoustic like John Lennon's Rickenbacker. Then, when protest music and demonstrations against the war came along, Yamaha put out a new and affordable type of folk guitar, and everybody scrambled to buy one of these. The guitar here in the Politicos' place wasn't a Yamaha, though, but a Yamasa, a name that sounded like a maker of instant soup or something.

After playing "Motherless Child" on the Yamasa, Iwase

did "Takeda Lullaby." Presumably he'd chosen these numbers because neither required more than two or three chords, but they were both mournful tunes, and playing them must have put him in a dismal mood because he now brought up a pretty depressing subject.

"You guys are both going on to college after you graduate, right?"

At the time, Adama still wanted to get into medical school at a national university; he didn't know yet that this would turn out to be an impossible dream. I don't remember exactly what I was thinking of doing, but I'm pretty sure I wasn't giving it all that much thought. I was already the sort of person who doesn't spend a lot of time contemplating the future. Not that I was indifferent about the meteoric drop in my grades, mind you—I was actually quite freaked out about it. The thought of ending up a failure scared me. This in spite of the fact that in 1969 failures were having a lot of fun: a high school student had published a book rejecting the whole idea of college education, Japanese hippies were pictured in magazines painting naked women with day-glo colors, and there were always a few beautiful chicks taking part in the demonstrations and marches. But you knew that couldn't last forever. In the long run, it's successful guys who get the women. I'm not talking about marriage or whatever; I'm talking about females in general, and lots of them. Unless a young man has some guarantee of getting his fair share of the fair sex, he can't go on living.

"What do you aim to do, Iwase?" Adama asked. Iwase was in a class made up mostly of hopeless cases.

"I don't know," he said. "I don't guess I'll be going to college. Ken-san, what about you?"

"I don't know, either. I might go to an art college, but ...
No, maybe I'll study literature.... Except, well, I don't know.
I haven't decided."

"You're lucky," Iwase said. He was strumming an A-
minor chord on the guitar. "You've got a lot of talent. Adama's got brains, too. I don't have anything."

I figured the reason he was being so gloomy had to do
with the sound of the **A-minor** chord, so I took the guitar away from him and started strumming a **G**.

"Come on, give yourself a break," Adama said gently
between sips of his coffee-flavored milk. "Look at John
Lennon. You read what he said in *Music Life*, didn't you? He
said he didn't have anything going for him at all as a kid.
You don't know if you've got any talent yet or not."

Iwase looked at the floor and smiled, as if touched and
embarrassed by Adama's attempt to cheer him up. Then he
shook his head.

"Believe me, I know. I can tell. But it doesn't matter.
You'll always be my friends, won't you? Both of you. Even
after we graduate?"

I realized now what was getting him down. He saw himself slipping into the background as Adama and I grew
closer. Before I met Iwase, he'd just been an ordinary,
below-average student, a softhearted kid on the soccer team
who was a major fan of some of the ugliest girls in school.
Then after we became friends he started reading the Beat
poets and listening to **Coltrane**, stopped following porkers around, and quit the soccer team. But it wasn't me
who'd changed his life; I was just the one who introduced
him to poetry and jazz and pop art and so on, and those are
the things that changed him. He fell under their influence

only because there was nothing to stop him from falling, and by now he knew a lot more about jazz and pop art and underground theater and poetry than I did. He'd always been my main man, my partner in crime. But since Adama had joined up with us, he must have thought his own role had become uncertain, and that buying us coffee-flavored milk was about the only thing he was good for.

You'll always be my friends, won't you? He looked really lonely when he said that. I hadn't seen him looking that way for a long time, not since we were first-year students. Back then we had a Classical Japanese teacher with a long, narrow face named Shimizu. Shimizu was a nasty bastard who used to rap us on the head with a wooden ruler if we fucked up on his exams: one whack for seventy points, two for sixty, three for fifty, four for forty, and so on. Iwase and a few other guys always got four or five whacks apiece. Toward the end of our second semester, as he was returning test papers, Shimizu said, "The year's almost over. We'll never finish the textbook if I have to spend most of my time hitting people. From now on I won't give anyone more than three whacks." Most of us were glad to hear this, but the worst students sort of stiffened. Shimizu gave Iwase his paper and said, "Lucky you, eh, Iwase?" That meant he'd got forty points or less, and we all laughed. Iwase just bowed his head and smiled his embarrassed smile, but, seeing how lonely he looked afterward, I realized he would probably have preferred being smacked on the head to being ignored.

"Oh!... Isn't Otaki here?"

The gloomy atmosphere Iwase had created was broken by the sound of a female voice. Two girls wearing commercial high uniforms—gorillas compared to Kazuko Matsui, but a million times better than no chicks at all—appeared in the doorway. They looked at Adama and giggled. Adama came in handy at times like this. Girls got the giggles when they met good-looking guys. It weakened their defenses.

So you could say things like:

"Hi! I'm Yazaki from Northern High, this is Yamada, that's Iwase. You're from the commercial high? Come on in. What's in the bag? Eh? Rice crackers? Open 'em up. Hey, we're all comrades, right?"

Their names were Teiko and Fumiyo—straight out of a melodrama about prewar factory girls. I rapped with them about Eldridge Cleaver and Daniel Cohn-Bendit and Franz Fanon, pointed out the similarities between Machiavelli's *The Prince* and the emperor system in postwar Japan, and argued about whether Che Guevara's activities in Bolivia exemplified the fundamental aims of anarchism. Which is all a lie, of course. Munching rice crackers, I picked out Simon and Garfunkel's "April Come She Will" on the guitar and explained how unhealthy it was for high school girls to remain virgins and how all the teachers at Northern High had given up on Otaki and Narushima because of their low IQs. The two factory girls, however, gave every indication of being the Politicos' squeezes; they went with the futon and pillows and tissue paper. I'd already heard that Otaki and Narushima went around dropping hints that joining their committee was a sure way of getting laid. So it was true. The slimeballs. Why didn't they take the cause more seriously? It made me sick, and so envious I could have wept.

I was just explaining that it wasn't an immutable fact that throwing water on mating dogs would make them separate, that there were exceptions, and had the two factory girls cackling with laughter, when Narushima and Otaki and a string of seven of their followers showed up. One of them was a college student wearing a helmet. The others were Fuse and Miyachi, two creeps from the debating team; a guy named Mizoguchi, who'd come within an inch of being expelled for swiping someone's bicycle; Masutabe, the owner of the eight-millimeter camera; and two other second-year students.

Narushima looked at me and smiled uncomfortably. They'd both been in my class in our second year. Neither of them did well in school. I was going around spouting about the evils of imperialism—without really knowing what I was saying, of course—before either of them knew Lenin from lemonade. They'd been your average lousy students in those days, just beginning to resign themselves to the fact that they weren't very bright. The Joint Campus Action Committee changed their lives: it showed them that even under-achievers could become stars. When they began sneaking leaflets into school from the Students and Workers Liberation Front at Nagasaki University, I still couldn't take them seriously, and even now I knew they felt inferior to me. But what with the futon and pillows and tissue paper and the fact that they had other backward types to push around, they seemed a bit more confident nowadays.

"What's this?" Narushima said. "What brings you here, Yazaki?"

"You want to join up?" Otaki asked. When he'd first come up with the idea of forming a JCA Committee at Northern High, I'd told him to count me out. I'd done a lot of soul-searching and decided that the time just wasn't ripe yet for that sort of thing. No, scratch that. I turned him down because I didn't like the idea of being punished by the school for joining a radical group, and, besides, I thought making films would be a shorter path to futons and pillows and tissue paper. But that was all beside the point now. This was for Kazuko Matsui. Bambi, my little fawn, liked men who rallied to the cause.

"Yeah, I want to join," I said.

Otaki and Narushima were surprised at first, then delighted. They shook my hand and introduced me to the guy in the helmet, saying I was a brilliant theorist who'd been reading Marx and Lenin since my junior year. Helmet said theory alone wasn't much use and gave me a look. He seemed like a jerk. I was dealing with nine people, though. I needed to **take control** in one swift move.

"All right, then. Otaki, let's hear your strategy for the struggle from here on," I said.

Otaki and Narushima looked at each other uncertainly. Fat chance they'd have anything like a course of action in mind. They didn't have the brains or the balls to actually do anything.

"Well, I don't know if you'd call it a strategy, but we're going to form a study group with people from Nagasaki U. and work on leaflets with the Peace for Vietnam Committee and try to get more recruits and—"

"Look," I interrupted, "let's barricade the school."

None of the high schools in Kyushu had ever been barricaded; it hadn't even been done at Nagasaki U. For people in a small city in the wilds of western Kyushu, tear gas and barricades were like Godard and Led Zeppelin—the stuff of dreams. Everybody was blown away by the idea.

"I've already decided the day. July 19, the last day of school. We'll barricade the roof."

"That's crazy," Helmet said. "Totally off the wall."

"Listen, pal, you keep out of this. This involves Northern High, not college boys who've never got around to taking any action themselves."

Masutabe and the other second-year kids looked at me, their eyes aglow with new respect.

"The problem is, we're talking about an organization with, what, less than ten members. We let them know who's behind it and we'll be expelled, just when we're getting started."

The more I talked, the more confident I felt.

"Until we get more people on our side, we've got to keep it all secret. Go underground. We'll barricade the place, but won't hang around. Hit them, and withdraw. Guerrilla tactics."

I was really rolling now.

"One of our tactics will be graffiti. We'll cover the walls with slogans. And we'll hang a giant banner from the roof. We'll block off the stairs and the entrance to the roof so they won't be able to take the banner down. We'll do it all late at night, in true guerrilla style. And, by the way, we're going to need a different name for the committee, otherwise Otaki and Narushima'll be kicked out in no time. As long as there's only a handful of us, we can't let anything like that happen. Che wrote something to that effect in

Guerrilla Warfare, I think."

Nobody said anything. Adama alone was smiling and nodding. He was the only one who knew this was all for Lady Jane's sake.

"With a group this small, it won't cost much to set it up. The reason we do it on the last day of school is that it'll make it harder for them to investigate, and it'll also have more impact on the students. They'll be coming to school feeling great because summer vacation's about to start. They'll see the banner, and they'll freak out. Then, during the vacation, since they won't have much contact with the teachers—less chance of having their minds warped by reactionaries—they might even read some Marx or think about the war in Vietnam. 'Smash the National Athletic Meet'—that'll be one of our slogans. The Athletic Meet is a counterrevolutionary ritual devised by the government to keep us all in line. There's a lot of bad feeling about it, too—girls are upset, for example, because all the practice for the opening ceremony interferes with studying for entrance exams. We use that. It's easier to expand the scale of the struggle if there's a concrete problem to focus on—one that people care about enough in private to fight against in public. Naturally we won't advertise the fact that any of this was planned by people at Northern High, but we won't say it was the work of outsiders, either. We'll *hint* that it *might* have been an inside job—that's about as far as we'll go."

Otaki raised his hand and asked me to hold on a second.

"What are we going to call ourselves, if not the JCA Committee?"

I told him not to worry. "I've already thought of a name:

53

Vajra. It's Sanskrit for the gods of lust and anger. Pretty cool, eh?"

"Far out!" shouted Masutabe, and everyone applauded.

And that's how I became the leader of Vajra, the new dissident movement at Northern High.

CLAUDIA CARDINALE

A few days after the midterm exams, which I'd screwed up badly on, I was climbing the hill to the hideout with Adama and Iwase.

"Ken-san," Iwase said, "you remember last year when we went to Hakata?"

"Sure. The time we spent the night in the movie theater, right?"

He was talking about one weekend the previous summer when he and I had taken a train to Hakata to see some films. We'd heard they were having an all-night Polish film festival.

"Remember the jazz place we went to?"

"Yeah."

"What was the name of it again?"

"Riverside Café, wasn't it? It was right beside a river."

"I'm thinking about getting a job there during summer vacation."

"At the Riverside? Oh, yeah?"

"Yeah. The owner was a nice guy, remember? I sent him a letter."

"Is that right?"

We'd set out for Hakata after lunch on a Saturday, skipping afternoon homeroom. First we went to Kyushu University to look at the wreckage of a Phantom jet that had crashed into one of the buildings there, then, after a bowl of noodles, we headed for the movie theater district. Right across the street from the little place showing **art films** was a marquee in bright primary colors. Adorning the marquee was a huge pair of pink boobs, and written on it were three titles: *The Angel's Entrails*, *The Fetus Poachers*, and *Inflatable Wives in the Wilderness*. I stopped and peered at it. Iwase saw what was coming and tried to drag me toward *Pasazerka*, *Mother Joan of the Angels*, and *Kanal*. "Wait wait wait wait, Iwase, that's a film by a great director, man—look, Polish flicks are fine but they're not even showing *Ashes and Diamonds*, we don't have enough money for a hotel, we're going to have to stay in the theater all night, and how are we gonna sleep with Polish partisans and nuns writhing in agony all over the screen?" Iwase, ever serious-minded, insisted we flip a coin, and I lost. I lost, but I told him I wasn't going to watch a bunch of fucking Nazis anyway and headed for the pink boobs. The next day, in the afternoon, we went to the Riverside Café to listen to some jazz. Iwase asked them to play a slow, moody piece by Coltrane, and I chose a bossa nova by Stan Getz. In between Coltrane and Getz they played something by Carla Bley, requested by a group of girls in their early twenties who worked in the ladies clothing section of a local department store. Salesgirls listening to Carla Bley—that was the late sixties for you. One of them was just Iwase's type. She was like the epitome of all junior-college-graduate department store salesgirls: plain and simple, with long hair, dark skin, and narrow eyes....

I knew she and Iwase had been writing to each other. The reason he wanted the job, I figured, was so that he could see her. He'd shown me one of her letters once: *Dear Hide-bo. How are you?* (Iwase's given name was Hideo.) *I'm listening to a session by Booker Little and Eric Dolphy as I write this. You're probably right about me being a weak person. I know I shouldn't care what people think, I should trust my own feelings. But when I think about all the people around me I just lose my nerve....* When I asked what she was talking about, Iwase played dumb and said he didn't know, but it was pretty clear to me that she was involved in some sort of **forbidden love**: a sales manager, married with kids; a yakuza; her stepfather; her pet dog—something along those lines, probably. If there was one area in which Iwase was more grown-up than I was, it was his connection with this chick. Whenever I mentioned her, he'd smile knowingly and mutter, "She's a real woman." I was jealous. For all I knew he might cross the line before I did. I remembered her sitting there in her thin dress. It was true, she did have a "real woman" sort of air about her; not like the whores with their cheap perfume who hung out in bars full of foreigners, but something that ordinary young women working in the real world had. Why should Iwase bring up the Riverside Café now, though, as we were walking to the hideout in the rain? "You're going there so you can see your salesgirl, right?" I said. "How'd you guess?" he said, nodding and giggling—if you could call that creepy sound a giggle. With Adama and me taking control of the Northern High JCA Committee, Iwase must have felt insecure about his own position, and this was probably his way of reasserting himself. A vision of that sweet-smelling salesgirl, naked, filled my brain. It pissed me off, and in my heart I shouted: *I hope she dumps you like a turd!* The hydrangeas along the road were just beginning to change color, and Adama, ignoring us, was poking at them with the tip of his umbrella.

Adama was cool.

"Power to the Imagination."

This was the slogan we decided to paint on the banner. Narushima and Otaki wanted it to be some cliché like **"Fight the Good Fight,"** but Masutabe and his classmates were overwhelmingly in favor of choosing one of the slogans Adama and I had taken from a collection of graffiti produced during the May Revolution in Paris—things like "Reject Preestablished Harmony!" and "Beneath the Pavement Lies a Desert."

It was fun thinking up slogans of our own. We all wrote them down on little strips of paper and read them aloud. Outside the window, rain was falling like fine silver needles. All we needed were conical straw hats and we'd have looked like Basho and his boys writing haiku.

"Ken-san," Iwase said, "the barricade's one thing, but what about the festival? What about the movie?"

On our way home from the hideout we'd stopped at a café called Boulevard where they played classical music. Iwase was drinking coffee. Coffee was the preferred drink of second-rate students in all small provincial cities in those days.

"We'll do 'em during the vacation," I said.

"That'll give us time to write a proper script," said Adama. He was drinking soda water. People who came from the sticks to small provincial cities had a thing about soda water in those days. He sucked noisily through his straw, then asked, "What kind of movie we gonna make, Ken?"

"I haven't decided yet, exactly."

I was drinking tomato juice. The hippest young people in small provincial cities always drank tomato juice in those days. That's bullshit, of course. Tomato juice was still a novelty, and most people wouldn't drink it because it tasted like tomatoes, or because it wasn't sweet, or because the color turned them off. I forced myself to drink it for the simple reason that I liked to draw attention to myself.

"I told you before, though, didn't I? That it'll be surrealistic?"

"Oh, yeah. You did."

"What was the music gonna be again?" Iwase asked.

"Messiaen."

It was around this time that I'd begun trying to perfect the art of fucking with people's minds. I'd figured out that when someone else was hogging the limelight, you could cut him down to size by bringing up a subject he didn't know anything about. If the other person knew a lot about literature, I'd talk about the Velvet Underground; if he knew a lot about rock, I'd talk about Messiaen; if he knew a lot about classical music, I'd talk about Roy Lichtenstein; if he knew a lot about pop art, I'd talk about Jean Genet; and so on. Do that in a small provincial city and you never lose an argument.

"It's going to be avant-garde, right?" Adama said, taking out a notebook and ballpoint pen. "Could you just give me a rough idea of the story?"

"Why?"

"Well, if we're going to shoot it this summer, we've got to start preparing now, right? Equipment, staff, props…"

Adama was a born production manager. I was impressed —impressed enough to tell him as much of the story as I'd thought up so far.

"It'll be like a combination of *Andalusian Dog* and *Scorpio Rising*.… We'll start out with a dead black cat hanging from a tree, and we'll pour gasoline over it and burn it up, tree and all, with smoke rising from the ground, all backlit, see, and then, *vrrrooom!*, three bikers come roaring out through the smoke, and…" It suddenly occurred to me that there was no place for Kazuko Matsui in a film like this. My little Bambi and surrealism didn't mix.

"Scratch that," I said.

Adama looked up from his notebook, where he'd written "Dead cat (black) / Gasoline / Three bikers," and said "Eh?"

"Scratch that—films like that are a drag. Wait a minute. Okay, here's what we'll do. We'll change the story completely."

Iwase and Adama looked at each other.

"Here we go. The first scene will be a meadow in the highlands, in the morning. With the mist still hanging in the air. Somewhere like the meadows up on Mt. Aso."

"The highlands? Morning?" Adama burst out laughing. "How do you get from a dead black cat to morning in the highlands?"

"Imagery, man, imagery. That's the important thing, pure images. You understand that much, don't you? Okay, the highlands. Then we'll have the camera zoom down to a boy holding a flute."

"Masutabe's camera doesn't have a zoom."

"Adama, put a sock in it. We'll worry about the details later, all right? So then the boy with the flute plays a tune. Something really beautiful."

" 'Daisy Chain'?"

"Right, that's good. Any time you get a good idea like that, I wanna hear it. Then, after that, the girl appears."

"Lady Jane."

"Right. She's wearing **white clothes**. Pure white. Not like a wedding dress, though, more like a negligee, something you can almost see through. We'll have her ride in on a **white horse**."

"Horse?" Adama, who was writing "Flute / White clothes (like negligee, not wedding dress)," raised his head and said, "A horse? A white horse?"

"Yeah."

"Forget it. How we gonna get a white horse?"

"Don't go all realistic on me, man. Imagery, imagery."

"Imagery or no imagery, you can't film something we haven't got. You're never gonna find a white horse—you can hardly even find a regular horse these days. Ken, how about a dog? The people next door to me have got a big white Akita."

"A *dog*?"

"Yeah, name's Whitey. He's big enough, he could probably carry a girl on his back if he had to."

"You have Kazuko Matsui come in riding on an Akita hound, everybody's gonna crack up. Listen, you prick, you trying to turn this into a comedy?"

"Hey, cool it, guys," Iwase said, and we stopped arguing immediately. Not because of Iwase's intervention, though. An almond-eyed Claudia Cardinale look-alike wearing a

Junwa uniform had just walked in. She sat at the table next to ours and ordered tea with lemon. While the man who ran Boulevard was taking her order, I asked him to play Berlioz's *Symphonie Fantastique*, with Zubin Mehta conducting. "Here we go again," said Iwase. "Mr. Debonair. Berlioz, Mehta—that's the only combination you know." "Fuck you," I said. "I know *The Four Seasons* by I Musici, too." Now it was Adama who was saying "Cool it, cool it." Claudia Cardinale stood up with a shopping bag in her hand and disappeared into the restroom. When she re-appeared, she was a different person: her hair was curled slightly inward to frame her face, she was wearing eyeliner and pink lipstick, her white and dark blue uniform had been transformed into a cream-colored dress, her black flats had become high heels, and the smell of nail polish hung in the air around her. We looked at her gleaming fingernails and sighed. She glared back at us and said, "What?" "Nothing, nothing," we muttered, shaking our heads feebly, and she sniffed, brandishing a High-lite Deluxe between her fingers and puckering her lips to expel a stream of blue smoke into the air, where it mingled with the first movement of *Symphonie Fantastique*. Ignoring Iwase, who was whispering "Don't do it don't do it don't do it," I turned to Claudia and said, "Would you like to be in a movie?"

"Whaddaya mean?"

"We're going to make an eight-millimeter movie. We'd like you to be in it."

Claudia laughed loudly, showing us a set of pretty pink gums.

"You guys're from Northern, aren't you?" she said, ignoring my question. She mentioned the name of a certain punk in Shirokushi's group and asked if we knew him. "Went to Aimitsu Junior High? Tall guy, kinda dreamy?"

We nodded, and she smiled and said to say hi to him. I asked her her name. It was Mie Nagayama. I'd leaned over to tell her a bit more about the movie when Iwase suddenly stood up, urging Adama to do the same, and they each grabbed one of my shirt sleeves and dragged me toward the door. Near the cash register we stepped aside to let three guys in the uniform of the industrial arts school pass. They all had **flattops**, high collars, and bell-bottom pants. They eyeballed us, and we did a quick about-face to avoid their gaze. It was the leader of a notorious Hardboy gang and two of his thugs. They sat down at Mie Nagayama's table. When Mie waved goodbye to us, the gang leader turned and gave us a look. We paid our check in a hurry, stepped outside, and sprinted about a hundred meters. "So that's Mie Nagayama," Iwase said, panting and wheezing. Apparently she was famous. It wasn't as if she was the gang leader's property, he explained—she didn't belong to anybody in particular, but she played around so much that she was always on the verge of being expelled. "Okay," I said, "it's decided. We'll use her in the opening act of the festival." Iwase glumly reported that the gang leader was in the kendo club and was in love with her. "He'll beat you half to death with a wooden sword, Ken-san. Forget it."

Adama laughed cheerfully. "Beaten to death with a wooden sword. Don't come crying to me if that happens."

The dreary rainy season came to an end. During a pool-cleaning session at school, I sneaked up behind the girls' post-menopausal P.E. instructor and pushed her into the

dirty water. Somebody snitched on me, and Cauliflower Aihara gave me thirteen hard ones across the face. On the achievement tests, Adama dropped eighty places. He'd been at the top in chemistry the year before, but this year he was down near the very bottom. The college entrance advisor yelled at me, saying I was trying to destroy the kid's future. (Adama's scores go down, and I get yelled at—I couldn't figure that one out.) Iwase had his heart broken for the third time in his high school career, by a spiker on the girls' volleyball team. As for Kazuko Matsui, I'd only had one more chance to speak to her, in the hallway at school. She asked me about *Bookends*. I stammered that I'd bring it next time, next time for sure. "Don't worry," said Bambi, with all the tenderness of an angel, "any time's fine." I had to make a success of the barricade at all costs, for my angel Bambi Lady Jane.

We were making good progress with the preparations. We would strike, as planned, the night before the end-of-school ceremony on July 19. We had the paint and a long roll of cloth for the banner, and the hideout was a hive of activity. The barricade required a total capital investment of 9,255 yen. Each of us chipped in a thousand.

"Everyone listen up."

I was about to give them the final rundown.

"We'll assemble at midnight, under the cherry tree by the pool. Whatever you do, don't come by taxi. Otaki? You'll walk from your house? Okay. Narushima, you're walking, too, right? Fuse? Miyachi? You're staying with Narushima? Good. Masutabe's place is an inn, so I want Mizoguchi, Nakamura, and Hori to spend the night there. Leave the house separately, don't walk together. Don't do anything to draw attention to yourselves. And just to remind you: we'll take the paint and wire, pliers, rope, and banner, one by one, to Masutabe's and Narushima's places beforehand. I want everybody to wear black that night. No leather shoes. Whatever we have left over—empty paint cans, extra rope, and so on—we'll take back with us. Yamada and I will call the newspapers."

Then, using **red paint** on the white cloth, I wrote "Power to the Imagination." It felt great.

Three days before the big event, Iwase came to our classroom to tell Adama and me he wanted out. In the deep shade cast by the glaring summer sun of Kyushu, he told us, with tears in his eyes, that the idea of a barricade just didn't agree with him. "I'm sorry, Ken-san, I'm sorry, Adama. I'll help set things up, and I'll help with the festival, but I don't like this barricade stuff…." The gist of what he was saying seemed to be that there wasn't any serious political motive behind it, that I was just doing it to look like a big shot. This really got me down, and I confessed as much to Adama when Iwase left. "What's the difference?" he said. "Who needs politics? We're doing it because it's fun, aren't we? Ken, if it's fun, that's enough." Even so, I could tell he felt as bummed out as I did.

And then **July 19** arrived.

POWER
TO THE IMAGINATION

I had to leave my house at eleven, and that wasn't easy to do. My mother and little sister and grandparents were all asleep, but my father was still up. He was watching the **"11 P.M."** show. Every night since this program began, he'd been staying up past his bedtime.

Our house, like most houses in Sasebo, was built on the side of a mountain. The only ones on the narrow strip of level ground belonged to the American military and a handful of people who'd got rich catering to them in one way or another.

With my father still awake, I couldn't risk going out the front door. The house stood on a slope, and the back door opened onto one of the long, narrow flights of stone steps that linked all the roads in the neighborhood. My room was on the second floor. First I had to tell my father I was turning in for the night. I knocked on the door of his studio.

"Goodnight, Father dear."

I guess you know I didn't really talk to him that way. What I actually said was, "Hey, I'm goin' to bed."

He's sitting there getting his jollies watching the bikini

girls on the "11 P.M." show, but he turns in his chair and fixes me with a solemn sort of look. "Already? Why?" he said, and started telling me about how when he was in middle school before the war he used to stay up studying till 4:00 A.M.; but then he stopped short, remembering what was on the TV screen probably, and, clearing his throat, said, "Ken, I don't want you doing anything to upset your mother." My heart stopped. Did he know what I was up to? No, he couldn't possibly, but … *I don't want you doing anything to upset your mother.* Shit. What a time to start preaching at me. I went back up to the second floor, changed my clothes, and climbed quietly onto the clothes-drying platform. There was a full moon. Being careful not to make a sound, I slipped into my basketball shoes. (We didn't say "sneakers" in those days, we called them *bashu*—short for basketball shoes.) From the platform I crawled down to the first-floor roof. Right in front of me was a little cemetery. A row of gravestones glistened in the moonlight at about the same level as the roof, being higher up the slope. I jumped down into the cemetery—or, rather, I jumped onto a gravestone. I wasn't what you'd call religious, but I felt a bit guilty doing that. I always used this particular grave when I sneaked out to go to cafés or a porno film or Adama's boarding-house, and I was sure the occupant would put a curse on me someday. When I was a little kid, my grandfather had a friend, a bald-headed old guy who'd been a commander in the navy. My grandfather had only been a lieutenant commander, so Baldy lorded it over him even then, more than a decade after the war had ended. Baldy would come over in the middle of the day to drink, and my grandfather would tipple right along with him. I liked Baldy because he always brought me a new picture book when he came. But he had a bad habit: whenever he got drunk, he'd step outside and piss in the cemetery. My grandmother hated that and always said he'd be sorry, that one of these days he'd be cursed and die; and then one day his heart gave out and he really did drop dead. I was convinced he'd had a hex put on him. So whenever I slipped out to the all-night porno flicks or whatever, I'd press my palms together as I stepped on the gravestone and say *Forgive me, forgive me, forgive me*, over and over again. I prayed this time, too, but it was different now. I wasn't going to a dirty movie; I was going to barricade the school. Revolution. Surely the spirits of the dead would let this one slide.

Everybody was there by **midnight**, standing under the cherry tree next to the pool. We divided into two teams: one to paint graffiti, and one to seal off the doorway to the roof and hang the banner. I was with the graffitists. So was Adama. It was more dangerous for the roof team: after barricading the door, they had to climb back down on ropes. I suckered Narushima, Otaki, and all but one of the other kids into taking the roof by telling them it was the most revolutionary part of the whole operation. Adama was afraid of heights, and I just didn't want to risk getting hurt.

We were all set to roll when Fuse, a dark and filthy-minded little guy said, "Wait a minute."

"What's the problem, man? We've just gone over everything."

A hesitant, lecherous smile spread over Fuse's face.

"It's just that, uh, well, you don't get a chance like this very often."

Chance?

"I checked a while ago, and it wasn't locked."

Locked?

"The girls' changing room. Can't we just take, like, five minutes and have a look inside?" He gave a horny little chuckle.

There was only one way to respond to this.

"Look, you fucking asshole, we're here on a sacred mission, and you want to peek in the **girls' changing room**? If that's where your head's at, man, the whole thing's a failure before we've even started."

But nobody said anything of the sort. We all agreed to Fuse's plan immediately.

A sweet fragrance wafted here and there inside the room. It wasn't that the whole place smelled that way. As you groped about in the dark, you'd suddenly get a whiff of the unmistakable scent of a young girl blossoming into womanhood. Nobody swims with their underwear on, which meant that girls got totally naked here—that's what all of us were thinking. Everybody was running their hands along the shelves against the wall. I told them to stop, that they were leaving fingerprints, but when Masutabe found a slip in the corner of a bottom shelf, they all went apeshit and began a frantic search for other things that might have been left behind.

It pissed me off that they weren't obeying my rule about wearing gloves, and I conferred with Adama.

"What are we going to do about fingerprints? They're all over those shelves."

"Relax. The cops don't have your prints on file unless

you've got a record, right?" Adama kept his cool even in the midst of mayhem. "You think they're going to dust for prints in the girls' changing room, then check them against every kid in school? No way. It's not like a murder or something."

"Ken-san…" Nakamura, one of the second-year students, stepped between us. "I'm sorry," he said in a very small voice, "but … I'm done for." He seemed on the verge of tears.

"Done for?" Adama tensed up. "What do you mean?"

"My fingerprints. I forgot my gloves, and my fingerprints are on those shelves."

"Don't worry. They're not gonna start poking around in a place like this. Even if they did, they wouldn't know whose prints they were anyway."

"They, they'll know mine. Our first year in junior high, we made salt, okay? As a science experiment. And I got sodium hydroxide on my fingers, and my fingerprints melted off. My brother said there's probably nobody else in Japan with hands like mine, he said I should go on that TV show **'To Tell the Truth.'** Almost everybody in my class knows about it. They call me 'Unprintable.' So I knew I had to wear gloves tonight, but when I touched that slip Masutabe found, I just forgot all about it, and now what am I gonna do?"

We reached out and felt his fingertips. Sure enough, the pads were smooth, like scar tissue.

"Amazing."

Eventually we stopped laughing, and Adama was able to persuade him there was nothing to worry about.

I had slipped into a silent reverie, reflecting that Kazuko Matsui changed her clothes here, too, when Fuse the Lecher found a wallet. He announced his discovery and shone his flashlight on it, waving it for everyone to see.

"You asshole!" I shouted, and even Adama the Cool clucked his tongue. A wallet was trouble. Whoever lost the thing was sure to report it, and somebody could end up searching the changing room. For all we knew, we might have left some clues behind: a piece of paper, footprints, hair. I told Fuse to put it back where he found it, but he just gaped at me with a moronic expression on his face and said he'd forgotten which shelf it was on. Otaki and Narushima said why bother, just rip it off, and Unprintable Nakamura suggested that if we found out who the owner was we could slip it in her locker later. We decided to look inside. It was your average girl's wallet, plastic, with a picture of Snoopy on the front. Inside were a couple of thousand-yen bills, one five-hundred bill, and a bus pass. We read the name on the pass and burst out laughing: it belonged to the post-menopausal P.E. instructor I'd pushed into the pool two weeks before. She was an unmarried woman with great sagging buns and jutting cheekbones. Our pet name for her was Fumi-chan. Also inside the wallet were coins, a button, a wrinkled business card, a movie ticket stub, and a photograph. The photo was a black-and-white shot of Fumi-chan as a young woman, standing next to a man with a face like a cucumber in an old Imperial Navy uniform. We all sighed. What could be more pathetic than a dried-up, saggy-assed, war widow P.E. teacher with two thousand five hundred yen in her wallet? "Pick a shelf and put it back," Adama said, and everybody nodded.

"Smash the National Athletic Meet."

I wrote this on one pillar of the school's front gate in

blue paint, slapping it on hard so it would sink into the rough stone surface. On the other pillar Adama wrote "Fight the Good Fight." I told him not to use corny crap like that, but Adama, cool as ever, said it was good camouflage, that it would make it harder to come up with a clear profile of the culprits.

We'd banned the use of flashlights inside the school grounds. In the front courtyard was a carefully tended flower bed and, above it, the V-shaped main building, looming up as a dark triangle in the moonlight. Just looking at the building made me sick. On the window of the teachers' room I wrote "Running Dogs of the Power Structure" in blue paint, except for "Dogs," which I did in red. There wasn't a cloud in the sky, but it felt muggy to me, and I'd begun to sweat inside my thick T-shirt. "To Arms, Comrades," I daubed on the wall of the library. Nakamura came up and whispered that the roof team had entered the school via the emergency exit next to the gym. "All right, let's go inside," I said.

As soon as we'd got in, I stopped, afraid of leaving any evidence behind: I'd let some drops of sweat fall on the concrete floor, and I waited for them to dry before moving on down a long corridor where the third-year science classrooms were. The graffiti team consisted of Adama, Nakamura, and me. "I'll probably never be this nervous again in my whole life," Nakamura sputtered through trembling lips. "Shut up, you asshole," Adama hissed. Though I was sweating, my own lips were bone dry and my throat was parched. We went past the teachers' room, the administrative office, and the principal's office to the front entrance. Most of the kids at school came in through these doors each day of the week. With large strokes of red paint, I wrote "Kill!" on the wall. Nakamura gasped and asked if that wasn't going too far. Adama hissed at him again and pointed off to the right of the entrance. The watchmen's room. There were two watchmen, an old guy and a young one. The light wasn't on, though; they'd probably watched the "11 P.M." show and gone to sleep. On the floor just inside the main doors I scrawled "You're All Brain-dead! Fuck Higher Education!" Nakamura began shaking like a junkie in withdrawal. He was squatting next to one of the columns, doing nothing to help. "This isn't cool," Adama whispered to me. I could tell he was nervous, too—he kept licking his lips. The building was absolutely silent, and the only light was from the moon, streaming in through the windows; it was like being on a different planet. The fact that this was a place we clattered through in a noisy crowd almost every day only made the tension worse. We pulled Nakamura to his feet and dragged him away from the entrance, as far as the door of the principal's office. Getting away from the watchmen's room was a bit of a relief, but now Nakamura was hyperventilating. "Asshole," I said. "Go back to the pool." Nakamura shook his head. "You don't understand. I … I …" Sweat was pouring down his face. "What? What is it?" Nakamura wagged his head again. Adama shook him by the shoulders. "Tell us. What is it? Ken and me are scared, too, man. There's nothing to be ashamed of. What's the problem?"

"I have to go **doo-doo**."

It wasn't fair: why should *his* bowel problems give *us* a stomachache? I rolled on the floor trying to smother my laughter, with my right hand over my mouth and my left holding my belly, heaving with hiccoughing spasms. Adama was doing the same. Tension only encourages laughter: it's never so hard to stop laughing as when you mustn't laugh. All we had to do was mutter "doo-doo" and the giggles would burst in our guts, then come bubbling up our throats. I closed my eyes and tried to remember the saddest things that had ever happened to me: the New Year's Day when my parents hadn't bought me the Patton tank model I'd wanted; the time my father had had an affair and my mother left home for three days; my little sister being hospitalized with asthma; the pigeon that didn't come back when I let it loose; the time I dropped my pocket money at a local festival; a penalty shootout in the prefectural junior high soccer finals, which our team lost. None of them worked. Adama had both hands over his mouth and was shuddering and wheezing. I'd never realized how hard it could be to control the giggles. I drew a picture of Kazuko Matsui in my mind: her slender, milky calves, her Bambi eyes, her white arms, the awesome curve of the nape of her neck—and the spasms finally stopped. Such is the power of beautiful women: they can even stifle laughter, make a man sober and serious. After a while Adama, too, stood up, drenched with sweat. He told me later he'd pictured the charred corpses he'd once seen after a mine explosion. Being forced to remember a scene like that must have made him angry: he rapped Nakamura on the head with his fist.

"Asshole. I thought I was going to lose my mind," I said and quietly opened the door to the principal's office. "Hey, Nakamura."

"Yes?"

"Is it diarrhea?"

"I don't know."

"Can you do it right away?"

"It's already poking its head out."

"Do it up there."

"Eh?" he said, and his jaw dropped. I was pointing at **the principal's desk**. "I can't do that."

"What do you mean, you can't do it? It's your punishment for making us laugh and nearly getting us busted. If we were real guerrillas, we'd have killed you right then and there."

Nakamura was close to tears, but we wouldn't let him off the hook. Bathed in moonlight, he climbed up onto the desk.

"Don't look, okay?" he said in a pitiful voice as he pulled down his pants.

"If you think it's going to get noisy, stop," Adama whispered, holding his nose.

"Stop? Once it starts coming out, I can't stop."

"You wanna get thrown out of school?"

"Can't I do it in the toilet?"

"Nope."

Nakamura's white ass shone in the moonlight.

"I'm too nervous. It won't come out."

"Push," Adama said, and that's when it happened.

Along with a little whimpering cry, Nakamura let out a tremendous fart. It sounded like a broken bagpipe. Adama ran up to him and whispered, "Keep it down! Plug up your ass with something!"

"It's too late," Nakamura said.

The noise was incredibly loud and seemed to go on forever. I got goosebumps all over and turned to look toward the watchmen's room. If we got expelled for a fart, we'd be the laughingstock of the school, but they still seemed to be asleep. Nakamura wiped his ass with the monthly newsletter of the Nagasaki Prefectural High School Principals Association, and smiled sheepishly.

The other team had nearly finished barricading the door to the roof with wire and desks and chairs. Otaki told us wistfully that it would have been even better if he'd had welding equipment.

Narushima and Masutabe were the only ones left on the roof. After securing the door from the outside with wire, they had to slide down a rope to a window on the third floor. We all watched them from the courtyard in front of the school. Narushima had been in the mountain-climbing club, so we weren't worried about him.

"What'll we do if Masutabe falls?" Otaki said. "Might as well decide that now."

"We'll call the cops and run." It was, of course, Adama who made this decision. "Hell, if we try to help him, we'll all be busted."

Masutabe, unlike Narushima, was swaying back and forth on the rope. Fuse said he wouldn't be surprised if the kid was pissing his pants. I told them about Nakamura's revolutionary bowel movement, and everyone doubled up laughing.

Masutabe somehow managed to make it down safely. The banner was hanging from the roof.

"Power to the Imagination."
We all stood silently gazing up at it.

JUST LIKE A WOMAN

At six o'clock in the morning, Adama and I made seven telephone calls: to the local branches of the *Asahi*, *Mainichi*, and *Yomiuri* newspapers, the main offices of both the *Western Japan News* and the *Nagasaki Post*, and the broadcasting stations NHK Sasebo and NBC Nagasaki.

The purpose of the calls was to issue a **communiqué**:

"Before dawn this morning, members of Vajra, the radical organization we belong to, carried out a successful mission to set up a barricade in one of the strongholds of the system's propaganda machine, Sasebo Northern High School."

That's what we'd intended to say, but since we were new to this sort of thing, it turned out more like, "Um, listen, it, uh … it looks like somebody barricaded Northern High in Sasebo, okay?"

It didn't matter, though. Thanks to this announcement, the mass media discovered the barricade and graffiti before the watchmen, the teachers, the students, or the people in the neighborhood.

NHK and NBC reported it on the 7:00 A.M. local news.

Too nervous and excited to sleep, I was lying in bed

checking for about the hundredth time that there weren't any paint stains on me, when my father, who'd just been watching the news, came into my room. There was a scary look on his face.

"Ken-bo," he said, using my childhood nickname. My parents had called me just plain "Ken" since around my last year of elementary school, but whenever relations between us were strained they reverted to "Ken-bo." Maybe it was their instinctive way of showing they missed the good old days when I was still a little kid. At any rate, I knew the barricade had been on the news as soon as I heard him call me this.

"Ken-bo, look me in the eye," he said.

My father had been an art teacher for twenty years. He frowned and peered at me, confident in his ability to tell when children were lying. I looked back at him with no sleep and the aftermath of intense excitement written all over my face, but apparently he decided I was innocent. Even a veteran teacher can be a pushover when it comes to his own kids. The fact that a lot of ultra-radicals were the sons and daughters of schoolteachers was often attributed to their strict upbringing, but the truth is that just behind that apparent strictness was a tendency to spoil them rotten. Teaching is a strange profession. It's like being an officer in the Self-Defense Forces, or a policeman. Though most people in these positions are just your average slobs, the general public—at least in the provinces—still treats them almost with reverence. This isn't something they've earned for themselves but a throwback to the prewar years, when respect was their reward for cooperating with the fascist system; and old habits die hard. As a teacher, my father had always been quick to resort to corporal punishment. It wasn't only students he got rough with, either: he'd been known to slug the principal at his school and the head of the PTA. He never hit me, though. I once asked why, and he said his own children were just so damned lovable he couldn't bring himself to hit them. He was an honest old guy.

"Okay," he said. "You didn't do it, did you."

I rubbed my eyes, pretending to be still half asleep. "What're you talking about?"

"Somebody barricaded Northern High."

I opened my eyes wide and sprang out of bed. I slipped on my trousers in three seconds, my shirt in four, and my socks in two. Seeing what a flap I was in seemed to make my father even more convinced of my innocence. I dashed downstairs and out the door, calling out to my mother that I didn't need any breakfast, and ran down the road at full tilt for about a hundred meters—then slowed to a saunter.

When I got to the bottom of the hill in front of the school, I could see the banner.

"Power to the Imagination."

It was a stirring sight. All on our own, we'd managed to change the scenery.

I climbed the hill with my heart pounding. The physics teacher and about a dozen students were at the front gate, trying to scrub off the graffiti. The smell of paint thinner filled the air. There was something downright disgusting about these kids in their eagerness to see the scenery return to normal. Someone from a radio station was interviewing them:

"Who do you think could have done this?"

"It wasn't anyone here. Northern High students wouldn't ever do something like this," said a disgusting girl with blue paint caked under her fingernails. Her voice was choked with tears.

When I got to the classroom Adama smiled at me and winked, and when no one was looking we shook hands.

Eight-thirty came and went, and **homeroom** still hadn't begun. Announcements over the P.A. system told us to wait in our classrooms, but the whole school was in pandemonium. Helicopters hovered overhead. One team of disgusting students was helping the P.E. instructors dismantle the stuff on the roof. Another object of disgust—the vice president of the student council—was working away with a thinner-soaked rag in an effort to erase the red "Kill!" I'd painted near the front entrance. When he spotted me, he dashed over. His eyes were red; he'd been kneeling there crying as he scrubbed at the paint. He grabbed hold of my collar with the hand that held the rag.

"Yazaki, it wasn't you, was it? Huh? You didn't do it, did you, you weren't the one, were you? I just can't believe any Northern student would do this to his own school, but tell me, come on, tell me you didn't do it, tell me, dammit, tell me!"

The rag he was holding was cold, and I didn't enjoy having it pressed against my neck. I considered punching him one, but I was afraid of drawing attention to myself, so I just glared at this four-eyed, buck-toothed runt, who at seventeen was already going gray, and yelled, **"Let go of me!"** I couldn't figure out how he could be so upset.

Somebody paints slogans on the walls of your school—is that something to start blubbering over? What was it to him, a holy shrine? People like this were dangerous, though. Very naive. It was people like this who'd murdered and tortured and raped in Korea and China. People like this cried over graffiti, but it was nothing to them if one of their classmates started sucking sailors' dicks as soon as she graduated from junior high.

"Ken, you backed down."

Adama had been watching my run-in with the vice president.

"No, I didn't. That asshole's really over the top, though."

"Yeah. It's amazing that a guy'd get down on the floor and scrub like that. Getting his hands sopping wet."

"I know. How can they get so intense about it? If I did back down, it was because the guy was, like, overwhelming."

"There was no fight in you, man."

"How come, I wonder."

"Because it wasn't 'the good fight,' maybe."

"What's that supposed to mean?"

"Our motives weren't exactly pure, right?"

"Our motives? For the barricade?"

"It's not like we were going to die or something if we didn't pull it off."

"What do you know about dying, Adama? Do you have any idea how many people are dying in Vietnam every day?"

Whenever I started spouting clichés like this, I'd suddenly find myself speaking standard Japanese. The kind of stuff the Peace for Vietnam Committee said in their speeches sounded funny in dialect, somehow.

"Vietnam, right."

"It was bastards like him who went berserk in Nanking and Shanghai and all those places."

"Nanking, right. But, listen, doesn't it make you feel sort of weird to see 'em going all out to clean up like that?"

"'Course it does. I didn't know there were that many supporters of the fuckin' system here, man."

"That's not what I mean."

"Oh?"

"I mean, it's like we created something for them to get all gung-ho about."

There was an air of sadness about Adama as he said this. He was always like that. He'd say things in a tone that suggested a sense of futility. But he really knew how to get his point across.

A great throng of students stood outside in the July sun, sweating as they worked to strip the graffiti from the windows of the teachers' room and the wall of the library. Maybe Adama was right: it wasn't only the honor students who were out there with cleaning rags but even the dimmest kids—kids who, thanks to this school, had such a low opinion of themselves they were practically suicidal.

Nakamura was standing outside the principal's office, looking as pale as a ghost. He, too, was holding a rag. When he saw Adama and me he gave us a tight little smile.

"What're you doing with that thing in your hand?" Adama said.

Nakamura licked his lips nervously.

"I didn't think it would be smart to just sit around. It'd look suspicious. Remember, I'm the guy they call **Unprintable**. But anyway, listen, Ken-san, it's really strange...."

"What is?"

Adama suddenly grabbed my sleeve, pulled me down to a squatting position, and started pretending to rub at the floor. Nakamura and I soon followed suit. Walking down the hall toward us were the guidance counselor, the two watchmen, the vice principal, a uniformed policeman, and another man who looked like a plainclothes detective. I glanced at the policeman and shivered. Why do cops jingle and jangle so much when they walk? He was wearing heavy lace-up shoes, and these also made a lot of noise. When the counselor's slippers stopped right in front of me, I thought my heart was going to burst. The cop's jingling and jangling and clumping stopped, too.

"You boys," the counselor said.

I looked up at him, feeling as if all the breath had been knocked out of me.

"You boys will never get the paint off by rubbing at it like that. We'll have some professionals come in to clean up. I understand how you feel, but I want you to go on back to your classrooms. Homeroom will be starting soon, and we're going to hold the closing ceremony as planned. Run along, then."

I was mad at myself for being so scared—I'd pictured us being arrested and strung up on the spot—but I felt a lot better when I saw the troubled expression on the counselor's face and the deep creases between his eyebrows.

This was the guy who'd caught me in a jazz café listening to Antonio Carlos Jobim, taken my glass of Coke away, slapped me forehand and backhand about ten times, and got me suspended from school for four days; the sort of bastard who got his rocks off preaching about the evils of delinquency, complete with quotes from Confucius or whatever, every time we had an assembly or ceremony of some kind. He was a tall guy with silver hair who'd written several books about criminal law in the ancient world, and his way of dealing out shit was as mean as they come. He wouldn't ever lose his temper, just eye you coldly and say, "You're trash, we don't have enough time to try to make a decent student out of you, so why don't you just drop out or find some other school if you don't like it here?" This was the prick who was now shuffling off toward the teachers' room with drooping shoulders and a gloomy face. I heard the vice principal say something about "the biggest **disgrace** in the history of the school."

In the history of the school. Adama and I grinned at each other and shook hands again.

Adama suggested we take a look at the roof. Nakamura came along with us.

"You were saying something was strange," Adama said to him as we climbed the stairs.

Students with rags swarmed around the columns we'd defaced at the top of the stairs.

"Yes, well, you see, it was sort of weighing on my mind, so the first thing I did when I got to school was check out the principal's office, and you know what?—it didn't even smell or anything."

"I'm not surprised. A turd'd be the first thing they'd clean up."

"Ah … now that you mention it, I did think I could smell disinfectant or something."

"Probably the watchmen. They would've been awake by six or so. After they found the graffiti, they must've freaked out and gone straight to the teachers' room and the principal's office. Soon as they saw that mess they'd have mopped it up. After all, a pile of shit is… Well, it's not exactly funny." Adama was as calm and logical as ever.

"Eh? What do you mean 'not funny'?"

"Nakamura," I said, "do you think there's any ideology in shit?"

"Ideology? In … shit? No, I guess not."

"Even back before the war, the secret police used to give political offenders at least a little bit of leeway, but people whose crimes weren't based on any sort of ideology, they'd crucify 'em just like that. And we're talking about *shit*, man. It's not only filthy, it's, like, unthinkable, totally insane."

"Wait a minute, Ken-san." Nakamura came to a halt halfway up the stairs. "You're the one who told me to do it!" he whimpered.

"How many high school students do you think would take a crap on a desk just because someone tells 'em to? Don't you know a joke when you hear one?"

By now he was almost crying. Adama put an arm around his shoulders and tried to calm him down.

"Ken's only kidding. He's just teasing you, man, take it easy."

As it turned out, the "doo-doo" incident never did come to light; it wasn't mentioned in the papers, the radio and television reports, or the police statements, and not even the principal ever referred to it, as far as I know. So the watchmen probably *had* cleaned it up, and decided to keep it their own little secret.

To get even with me, Nakamura said, "Ken-san, it was you who wrote 'To Arms' on the library wall, wasn't it?"

"Yeah, that was me."

"You got the characters wrong."

"Eh?"

"You used the one for 'exams' instead of 'arms.' Everybody was talking about it. They said it couldn't have been a Northern student because if anybody here was that stupid, all they'd need to find out who did it would be a **spelling test**."

Adama burst out laughing. Nakamura looked a bit happier, too.

They'd nearly finished breaking through the barricade. Aihara was cutting the wire with pincers, and Kawasaki was pushing aside the chairs and desks that were piled up against the door. Both were drenched with sweat. Aihara stopped what he was doing, looked at me, and grinned.

"Yazaki. What're you doing here?"

This was one fucker I wasn't about to grovel in front of. I didn't want to tell him some cowardly lie like "I've come to help dismantle the barricade," and, in any case, my scorn and loathing for the prick would have shown on my face and given me away.

87

"I just wanted to see what a barricade looks like. Sir."

Aihara's grin vanished and he glowered at me.

"It wasn't you, was it?" Kawasaki said. His shirt was stuck fast to his skin. I tried to dodge the question with a smile, but my cheeks twitched and it didn't quite come off. Luckily, at this point almost all the teachers thought the barricade had been the work of outsiders.

"Fnff," I went, in an attempt to laugh through my nose.

"If I find out you were involved in this," Aihara said, "I'll strangle you."

In one of the corridors I ran into Lady Jane, walking along with her hands clasped behind her back, humming "Just Like a Woman." She smiled at me. I was relieved to see that she wasn't carrying a rag and sweating—which meant, of course, that she hadn't been helping remove the graffiti. "Good morning, Yazaki-san," she said in a high, clear voice like a spring breeze. She left a scent of lemon shampoo behind her as she went by. Courage welled up inside me. I was proud, really proud, of what we'd done.

From in front of the main building I watched the banner being taken down. Aihara and Kawasaki rolled it up and stuffed it, along with its legend, into a big cardboard box.

Helicopters hovered in the air, and above them powerful cumulonimbus clouds marched through the clear blue sky of July. Our barricade had lasted less than half a day, but it seemed as if even the clouds and the sky were on our side.

It was on the third day of summer vacation that it happened, as I sat at home sucking a popsicle and watching a rerun of some melodrama on TV.

Four detectives paid a visit to my house.

ALAIN DELON

Detectives always turn up without any warning. "Hello, I'm a police officer and I'm on my way to your house to arrest you, so please be sure to be there"—that's something you'll never hear. Anyone who's had a visit from them has discovered an important fact about life: namely, that misery grows up all by itself, in a hidden place, without your even being aware of it, and then one day, suddenly, it knocks on your door. Happiness is just the opposite. Happiness is a cute little flower on your veranda, or a baby canary. You can see it growing, little by little, right before your eyes.

It had been mild and sunny all morning. Everything was the same as usual; the TV shows were the same, and the wedge-shaped popsicle I was licking had the same sticky sweetness. When the doorbell rang, my mother went to see who it was. There were four men outside, and they didn't come in. My mother, looking a bit shaken, called for my father. I still didn't realize what was going on. The men didn't look as if they'd come to collect on the gas bill, though, and I had a **bad feeling** about them. A bad feeling is like a thin, cold mist that hangs in the air, then suddenly thickens into a definite shape. One of the men was looking through the doorway at me. My parents turned and looked at me, too. The mist grew thicker. My mother sank to her knees on the carpet, and my father walked over to where I was sitting.

"Those men are detectives," he told me. "They say you're a suspect in the barricading of Northern High, and they want to take you with them."

I couldn't taste the popsicle any more. The mist was thick as soup. My brain went numb. I'd been found out. But how? Doubts and anxieties whirled around inside me, and my throat was bone dry.

"I told them it must be some sort of mistake, but ... Well, Ken? Did you do it?"

The popsicle was melting and dripping on the floor.

"Yeah, I did it."

"Ah."

My father stared at the little drops on the carpet for a few seconds, then walked back toward the detectives with a pained look on his face.

A police station is like nowhere else on earth. You could compare it to a teachers' room in the worst sort of high school, but even that would be stretching things.

I walked into the interrogation room muttering to myself *I know nothing I know nothing I know nothing I know nothing I know nothing.* Sitting across the shabby desk from me was a detective named Sasaki who was in the early stages of senior citizenship. When our eyes met he smiled and chuckled quietly. There were bars on the windows. Sasaki's shirt was open to his chest, and he was waving a fan with a peacock painted on it. It was hot. The sweat ran down my forehead and cheeks and neck, and it was all I could do to keep wiping it off.

"You hot?" Sasaki said.

I didn't answer.

"I'm hot, too. Your pals—Yamada, Otaki, Narushima—they told us the whole story." Sasaki took out a Hi-lite and lit up. "They all said you were the leader. That true?"

I was really thirsty. The sticky sweetness of the popsicle was still in my throat.

"You're not going to talk?"

Another cop came in with two glasses of cold barley tea and set them down in front of us. I didn't touch mine; I was afraid to. I somehow felt that if I drank it, I'd end up telling them everything.

"I see. Well, then, this is going to take some time. Yamada and the others'll probably be back home by noon or so. You're going to stick it out, though, huh? Look, you're only seventeen, and technically you're here of your own volition. We probably won't hold you overnight even if you don't cooperate. We'll get you to come back tomorrow morning. By then we should have the other statements all sorted out, and maybe we'll **arrest** you."

When I'd left the house, my father had said, "Ken-bo, the police know everything. Be honest with them—as honest as you can be without squealing on your friends—and hurry back home. It's not as if you killed someone, after all." I was impressed to see him remain so calm while his son was being dragged off by the cops.

"Listen, Yazaki, we're the police, it's our job to do this sort of thing. You understand? We sit in hot, cramped little rooms like this talking to suspects, and they're not all high school kids on their way to Tokyo University, either. Yeah, I spoke to your teacher—Mr. Matsunaga? He says you're pretty smart."

It doesn't take the police any time at all to get the goods on you. Misery develops before you even know it's coming, like a cavity in a tooth.

"They aren't all people like you. We get hoods, bums, hookers who're half out of their minds, junkies who you can't make head or tail of what they're jabbering about.... It tires you out. Hot in the summer, freezing cold in winter.... I've got neuralgia, it's no fun for me, but what can I do? One, two in the morning, you just want to get the hell out of here, but if it's your job, well, that's all there is to it. You're studying for college entrance exams, right? That's no fun, either, I know.... You still don't want to talk? You can come back tomorrow morning at eight, then. And if you keep this up tomorrow, we're going to have to arrest you."

I have no idea what the expression on my face was like right then, but I know I was feeling pretty depressed, and the whole business was beginning to seem ridiculous. The trouble was, I had nothing to fall back on, no stand I could take. All I could rely on was the anti-authority thing, the idea that whatever I did I wasn't going to play along with the fucking cops. But the urge just to get out of that awful place was gradually gaining the upper hand.

"You know how we found out?"

I shook my head. Drops of water ran down the sides of the cheap plastic glass of barley tea and soaked the peeling surface of the desk. How was a high school student supposed to know that the gloomy atmosphere of interrogation rooms was meant to be that way, to help break down the resistance of suspects and witnesses? A seventeen-year-old from a middle class family had no way of understanding that confessions were obtained by whittling down a person's pride bit by bit. All I knew was that I wanted to go home and enjoy a popsicle the way they were meant to be enjoyed.

"You don't know, do you? We couldn't have found out unless somebody talked, right? Well? You agree?"

My pride was slipping. I searched around for something to latch on to. When was it I'd gone with my father to see *The Battle of Algiers*? The rebels in **Algeria** didn't break down and confess even when blowtorches were used on their bare backs. It was better to die than to betray your comrades.... But what did that have to do with me? All I wanted was to go home and suck on a popsicle. Was this Algeria? Was the man in front of me a member of the French secret police? Was I fighting a war of national independence? Would it mean someone's life if I talked?

"Look at this." Sasaki pointed at a stack of papers on the edge of the desk. "Your friends' reports, with all the details."

That got to me. *All* the details? Did Nakamura tell them about the pile of shit? About Yazaki making him take a dump on the principal's desk? I was getting scared. It was just as Adama had said: a turd wasn't funny. There was no ideology in shit. I'd read a lot of accounts of student protests, but I didn't remember any of them listing defecation as a tactic. It wasn't so much that I was afraid of the charges against me becoming more serious; I was afraid of being treated **like a pervert**. There was nothing romantic about a turd....

"We already know the story, whether you talk or not.

Your pals told us everything. So now let's hear it from you. Come on, don't be stupid. You trying to cover up for somebody? You going to cover up for the clowns that told us they were only following your orders? Does that make you feel good or something?"

The things he was saying weren't very different from what was going through the mind of the popsicle fan sitting opposite him. He'd mentioned Adama's name. Adama was the only one I could trust. I had no ideological ties with the others; they were different, they were underachievers, and the only reason they'd gone ahead with the barricade was to try to boost their own feeble egos. I couldn't bear being lumped together with dickheads like that—they made it all seem meaningless. Algeria and Vietnam were far away. This was Japan, the land of peace. Sure, we heard the roar of Phantom jets every day. An ex-classmate whiled away her time sucking black sailors' dicks. But no blood was being spilled. No bombs were being dropped. No babies were scarred by napalm. So what was I doing here in this steaming shithole of a room at a police station in a little city on the western edge of a country like this? Was I going to change the world by holding my tongue? The radical movement was already in a shambles even at Tokyo University. I wanted something to hold on to, some grounds for opposing this wrinkled, cloudy-eyed old guy in front of me. I could say "I hate your guts!" and stick out my tongue—but that was about all I could do. The part of me that longed to be sucking on a popsicle kept asking questions: *Why did you barricade the school? You're not an Algerian rebel or a Viet Cong or one of Che's guerrillas. What are you doing here?* I knew damn well I'd done what I'd done because I wanted Kazuko Matsui to like me, but somehow it was hard to respect that as a motive now.

Sasaki shifted in his seat. He sat up straight and gave me a dour look.

"You hoping to become a bum, Yazaki? I've seen a lot of 'em, you know. Homeless guys that just wander around with nowhere to go. Maybe you were cut out to be one of them—you seem to like that free and footloose way of life, right? I know a lot of people who've gone that way. Yeah, you remind me of some of them. You know, there aren't many stupid beggars. 'Course, once they become beggars they start losing their marbles, but most of them planned at one time to go on to some good university—Tokyo, Kyo-to, that kind of place. Yeah … it's just that something goes wrong, some little thing, they make one little mistake and the next thing they know they're living on the street. They stink something awful, you know, those people."

I drank some barley tea. Then I threw in the sponge.

It was past eleven that night when I got home. Popsicles were the last thing on my mind. My parents didn't say anything at all for quite a while, but my little sister got out of bed in a cute pair of piggy-print pajamas to welcome me back. "You were out late, weren't you?" she said. "There's an Alain Delon movie I want to see. Will you take me?" Either she didn't know anything or she was just trying to brighten up the atmosphere. "Yeah, sure, I'll take you," I said, forcing a smile, which got me an "Oh, goody!" and a kiss on the cheek.

When she was back in bed again, my father muttered, "Alain Delon, eh?" He had his arms crossed and was peering at the ceiling. "What was that movie with Alain Delon and Jean Gabin? You and I and your mother went to see it together a few years back."

"*Mélodie en Sous-Sol*," my mother said. You could still see where tears had run down her cheeks.

"Right, right."

My father fell silent again for several long minutes. At times like this, the ticking of a clock is as loud as a drum. An odd little thought popped into my head: no matter what sort of shit is happening, time just keeps on passing by.

"Ken." My father turned suddenly and looked at me. "What if you get **expelled**?"

Obviously the two of them had done some talking while I was gone.

"Well, I'll take the high school equivalence exam. I'll go to college anyway."

"Yeah," he said quietly. "All right. Go to bed."

"The police contacted us yesterday. This isn't a problem that can be dealt with just by reading you the riot act. The principal will announce your punishment once it's been decided. At any rate, try to keep your noses clean till then."

It was the morning that summer supplementary classes were due to begin. Matsunaga, the guy in charge of our class, had called Adama and me into the teachers' room. There was a strange atmosphere in the place. It was nothing like when you were discovered smoking in the john or got caught cutting an exam to go and listen to some jazz. The teachers were cold and distant. "You again, Yazaki? You jerk. Why don't you try getting called in here for doing something right once in a while?"—nobody said anything like that. The P.E. instructors and the guidance counselor sat at their desks across the room and stared at us. Some of the teachers even looked down at their desks when our eyes met. I suppose they just didn't know how to deal with the whole thing. After all, it was the biggest disgrace in the history of the school....

It was the same in the classroom. The other kids were reading *The Pillow Book of Sei Shonagon*, trying to look as if nothing had happened. People like Adama and me were as much of a puzzle to them as to their teachers, here in darkest Kyushu. Between classes, a few close friends gathered around the two of us. I started talking in a loud voice about how much fun it had been. I told them about the planning, the execution, and the police interrogation, playing it up for laughs. The part about Nakamura's "doo-doo" was punctuated by one burst of laughter after another, and the crowd around us grew till it included about half the kids there. Telling the story made me a **star**. I learned something from that. If you got all gloomy and apologetic, you'd be on your own. No one there was capable of judging the right or wrong of it all. No one was capable of assessing the barricade in ideological terms. Victory went to whoever had the most fun. Behind the blasé front, of course, I was afraid of being expelled, but to put everyone else at ease it was best just to shrug it all off and tell them what a ball we'd had. The fact is that most of that crowd—or at least half of them—would have liked to have done it themselves. The rest, no doubt—the ones who thought I should get down on my knees and beg for mercy—only hated me more than ever. Aware of their hostility, I kept on talking. *Even if I am thrown out*, my heart was warning them, *you're the ones who lose. My laughter will ring in your ears for the rest of your miserable lives.*

After class, Adama, Iwase, and I had a talk in the library.

"How did they find out?" Iwase asked.

"Fuckin' Fuse," Adama said. "Fuse lives way out in the suburbs, right? The dumb fuck rode his bicycle home in the middle of the night with paint splattered all over himself. So a cop stops him. Nobody rides a bike around in the middle of the night way out in the sticks except a burglar or something, right? If he'd come up with a good story—I mean, country cops don't know shit, right? It would've been easy as hell to bullshit your way out of a situation like that. But Fuse starts babbling and screws everything up. At that point the cop's got no reason to suspect he's coming back from barricading the school, of course, but he asks Fuse his name and the name of his school just in case, because he's acting so suspicious. Once he heard the news—I mean, even the dumbest cop is going to start putting two and two together. They picked Fuse up right away, and he just spilled his guts."

"Yazaki-san."

It was the voice of an angel behind us. Kazuko Matsui was standing there with a concerned look on her face. Right beside her was Yumi Sato, the Ann-Margret of the English Drama Club.

"I was talking it over with Yumi-chan. We're thinking about starting a **petition** ... against them kicking you out of school."

If I'd been a dog, I would have rolled around on the

floor, pissed all over myself, foamed at the mouth, and wagged my tail till it snapped off.

LYNDON JOHNSON

All the third-year girls were assembled on the main playing field to practice for the opening ceremony of the National Athletic Meet. Supervising them was the war widow, Fumi-chan. Instructors at driving schools are the worst example of it, but all teachers get off on using their positions to intimidate the people in their charge. That's their way of trying to fill up the voids in their own lives. Dark, lonely lives create sadistic teachers.

"You there, you three girls! There aren't any boys watching you. The only reason you're not lifting your legs high enough is because you're worried about how you look. Nobody's looking at your silly legs. Lift them higher!"

Fumi-chan was shouting through a bullhorn. Adama and I were in low spirits in spite of the fact that we were gazing down on a sea of seventeen-year-old girls, about three hundred of them altogether. The principal was going to announce our punishment the following day. Lady Jane and Ann-Margret's idea of organizing a petition had never got off the ground. The school authorities had got wind that something was up and applied pressure before anything could happen.

After summer school two days before, I'd been discussing Jimmy Page and Jeff Beck with Adama and some other friends. We were trying to decide which of them could play faster, then which could run faster, which could eat faster, and so on. I said I bet that even when Janis Joplin farted, it came out sounding raspy, and everybody laughed. Then one guy suddenly stopped laughing and pointed at the entrance to the classroom, and we all fell silent. An **angel** was framed in the doorway, looking in our direction.

"Yazaki-san, do you have a minute?" she said, lowering her eyes. I floated toward her, suppressing an urge to start singing "My Little Butterfly." The angel stepped out into the hallway, leaned weakly against the wall with her hands behind her back, and looked at me with her head slightly bowed. *I'd do anything*, I thought, *even march off to war, to be the focus of those eyes*.

"Yazaki-san, I ..." The angel spoke in a tiny voice. To hear her, I had to move closer, close enough to smell her shampoo. I went into a sort of trance, gazing at the tiny beads of perspiration on her forehead, the fine wrinkles on her pink lips, and the flutter of her long eyelashes, wondering what it would be like to kiss that lovely oval face. The others were in the classroom doorway, peering out at us. Adama was grinning. Another guy flashed an obscene gesture, making a fist and poking his finger inside.

"Shall we go, like, to the library or someplace?" I suggested.

"This is fine," she said. "The thing is, well, Yumi-chan and I, and some other friends, we were going to start a petition, but our teacher said he wanted to see us, and, well, I'm so embarrassed, I didn't think I'd be able to tell you this, but

I know it would keep bothering me if I didn't, so I want to apologize because ..."

I saw it all. The teachers had threatened her. Talk about sadistic. I could imagine exactly how they'd gone about it; their methods were basically the same as the ones the cops and the secret police used. The entire system was on their side. "What's your problem? Let's hear it. Living in a free and peaceful country like this, going to a school with the best college entrance results in the prefecture, getting on with your studies to help you prepare for the future ... what have you got to complain about?" This would have been their line of attack.

"I'm sorry." She was biting her lower lip, unable to forget, presumably, the way they'd bullied her. I could have murdered them for this. The only thing that turned those bastards on was **stability**. "Getting into college," "getting a job," "getting married"—all their arguments were based on the premise that these things alone could lead to happiness. And it wasn't easy to deny a premise like that, at least for high school kids who hadn't yet found any real identity of their own.

"You're in class C, aren't you?" I said.

She nodded.

"Who's in charge of it? Shimizu?"

"Mr. Shimizu, yes."

Shimizu was the nasty bastard with the pointed chin whose profile looked like a crescent moon. I started doing an imitation of him. "Matsui, what on earth are you up to? Eh? How can you want anything to do with that slob Yazaki? Eh? You'd better think this over carefully. Eh?" Shimizu had graduated from the department of Japanese Literature at Saga University, the drabbest department in the drabbest university in Japan. Saga Prefecture had a Fountain of Seven Colors in front of its capitol building, the ruins of an old castle, and about a million miles of nothing but rice paddies. It was hard to find a decent bowl of noodles, or a woman under ninety, anywhere in the area. No one can tell me a guy who studied Japanese Literature in a dismal place like that had any right to say anything at all to a brave and beautiful girl like Kazuko Matsui.

My imitation of Shimizu wasn't very good, but she covered her mouth with her hand and giggled.

"Oh, I almost forgot," I said. "Wait here a minute."

I went back into the classroom and whispered to a guy named Ezaki, whose father ran a chain of beauty parlors, that I wanted to borrow the record he'd just shown me. Ezaki frowned and said "But, but, but—" "No buts, asshole, just hand it over," I said and glared at him till he opened his bag and pulled out his brand-new copy of *Cheap Thrills*. "But I haven't even listened to it yet," he moaned. I ignored him and ran back to where the angel was standing. Adama was telling Ezaki: "Forget it, man, let it go. When Ken's like this, it wouldn't matter if you were a cop, or a teacher, he'd walk off with the thing anyway. It's fate, man, let it go."

"You like Janis Joplin?" I asked her.

"Oh, I know this record. The lady with the husky voice, right?"

"Yeah. It's a good one."

"The only singers I know much about are the ones who came out of folk—Dylan, Donovan, Baez, people like that. But I know this record. 'Summertime' is on it, right?"

Lady Jane was a sweetheart. She didn't even mention Simon and Garfunkel, whose record I'd promised to give her and still hadn't produced.

"It's for you. Look, don't worry about the petition. I don't think we're going to be expelled anyway."

"This hasn't been opened! You haven't even listened to it yet, have you?"

"Doesn't matter. I'm going to be under house arrest or suspended or whatever, so I'll have plenty of time on my hands. I'll listen to it then."

I stared out the hall window at the mountains in the distance, wearing what I hoped looked like a lonely smile. Lady Jane still had her head bowed slightly and was peering at me from under her eyelashes. When I saw the look in her eyes I knew I'd pulled it off, and I felt like dancing up and down the hallway. The angel left, turning to look back at me several times as she walked away. Joining my friends again, I found Ezaki muttering darkly about people who only thought about themselves, but Adama said, "Way to go, man. You played it perfectly."

Now, with the drive to save us from expulsion having fizzled out, all we could do was wait for the principal's verdict.

"I wonder why watching this stuff makes me so sick," Adama said about the scene below, where girls were running up and down the chalk lines and jumping around in time to the music. I'd never seen Adama looking this edgy before—he was usually so cool-headed and laid-back. He never showed any anger or disgust or sadness in front of other people. It's true he came from a coal-mining town in the middle of nowhere, but his father had a job in management and his mother was from a good family and had graduated from higher school. Adama grew up with all the love and material comforts a kid could ask for. He'd even taken organ lessons till the age of five—something that in the world of coal miners practically qualified him as a member of the aristocracy.

This Adama of ours was really down now, though. The decision about our punishment must have been weighing pretty heavily on him.

Fumi-chan's shrill voice—"No, no, no! How many times do I have to tell you?"—grated on our ears. Blue and red veins stood out on her scrawny neck, and she was jiggling her ass in exasperation. What right did someone like that have to act so high and mighty? I didn't need Adama to tell me how sickening it was—I already felt like **puking**. There were, admittedly, some grotesque specimens among them, but to see seventeen-year-old bodies being ordered around was disgusting. Seventeen-year-old bodies weren't put on earth to be dressed in colorless gym clothes and forced to march around in some prearranged pattern. A few of them looked like hippos, it's true, but most seventeen-year-old bodies, with their smooth, elastic flesh, were designed to go running along some seashore playing tag with the waves and shouting with glee.

So it wasn't only the verdict, just one day away now, that was getting us down; watching the girls practice their routines was depressing, too. Just to see people being bullied into doing things was a bummer.

Neither of my parents mentioned the punishment question during dinner. When the meal was over, I went outside in my yukata to set off fireworks with my little sister. She told me she was going to invite a classmate she called Tori-gai-san over to our house soon. Torigai-san was half Ameri-can and strangely sexy for a sixth-grader. I was always after my sister to introduce me to her. The reason she remem-bered and brought it up now was that she somehow must have sensed, in spite of my attempts to fool around and be cheerful, how low I was really feeling.

My father was standing on the veranda watching us. He stepped down into the garden in his bare feet and said, "Let me give it a try." He took three sparklers in one hand, lit them, and waved them around in a circle. My sister clapped her hands, saying it was beautiful.

"Ken, about tomorrow," he said. I was busy painting a mental picture of Torigai-san's blue eyes and budding breasts and didn't realize at first that he was referring to the announce-ment. "I'm not going with you. I'll ask your mother to go along. If I went, you know, it could end up in a fight."

This was no surprise. Whenever the school summoned my parents, it was always my mother who showed up. I pre-ferred it that way, too. I didn't want to see my father stand-ing beside me apologizing for something I'd done.

"Look them in the eye," he said. "When the principal's dressing you down, don't look away or bow your head. I don't want you groveling to those people. There's no reason to swagger, but you don't need to be obsequious, either. It's not as if you killed anybody or held someone up or raped them or something. You believed in what you were doing, and now you've got to take the consequences."

I felt tears brimming up. Ever since the bust, we'd been under constant attack by adults. My father was the first to offer any sort of encouragement.

"If the revolution comes, you boys could end up being heroes, and the principal could be the one hanging from a rope. That's the way these things go."

He started waving the sparklers around again. Sparklers burn themselves out in no time at all....

But they're beautiful.

This was the first time I'd ever passed through a school gate with my mother at my side. Even at elementary school, it had been my grandfather who accompanied me to the opening ceremony—my parents couldn't go because they were both teaching.

On the way in, we met Adama's mother. She was tall, with features a lot like Adama's but more firmly molded. My mother bowed to her, saying, "I don't know how to apologize for all the trouble my son has caused you." I pulled her aside and whispered, "What the hell're you doing? You don't have to apologize to Adama's mother." Her reply was that even as a little boy, I was always the ringleader; "It's become part of your character," she said. Adama's mother looked at me with eyes that said *So this is the boy who led my dear little Tadashi astray*, but I smiled and gave her a cheerful "Hello! I'm Ken Yazaki." That was part of my character, too.

The principal's ruling was **"Indefinite confinement at home."**

" 'Indefinite,' of course, doesn't mean forever," he told us. "The period of time will be determined according to the extent to which you are judged to have shown regret for your behavior. Your graduation and admission to college depend on this, so we strongly advise you to avoid any further lapses and hope that both you and your parents will give some serious thought to the reasons for this situation."

"He wasn't expelled," my mother told my father over the phone, tears running down her face. The word "confinement" made me think of solitary confinement, which was pretty depressing, but the realization that our punishment actually meant I could ditch school without even being sneaky about it cheered me up a lot.

As we were walking back to the front gate, Yuji Shirokushi, the head Greaser, stuck his head out the window of a classroom in the middle of a supplementary lecture and shouted, "Ken-yan! Adama! What happened?" My mother got all flustered and flapped about in front of me, telling me to behave myself, but I ignored her and shouted back in a voice that echoed all around the courtyard: "We didn't get expelled! We're confined to our homes!" The members of my band, and the kids in our class, and Masutabe's supporters in the second year, and Shirokushi's Greaser underlings, and, and, and, and, and, and Kazuko Matsui, all looked out the windows of their various rooms and waved. I waved back—to Lady Jane.

Confinement at home technically meant that you weren't supposed to step outside your house at all, but since that was likely to drive anyone nuts and undermine the rehabilitation process, we were allowed a minimum of freedom referred to as "neighborhood outings."

I didn't miss anything much. I couldn't go to any movies or jazz cafés, of course, but my house wasn't far from the center of town, so I managed to keep myself amused, sucking popsicles and playing with our dog in the park and the area near the base, visiting bookstores and record shops, spying on the house where the groupies tangled with their sailor boys, and meeting my sister's friend Torigai-san.

Adama's situation was hell compared to mine. He'd had to leave his boardinghouse and move back home. The coal mines were on the verge of closing down because of an economic slump, and the place was practically a ghost town. They had a shoe store, a dry goods store, a stationery store, and a clothing store, and that was about it. Just about the only things in the clothing store were white cotton socks, the stationery store had nothing but rag paper, there was no instant curry in the dry goods store, and all the shoe store had in stock were split-toed canvas workshoes. Rumors that the mines were to be closed had been circulating for a couple of years now, and people were leaving in droves. All you saw on the streets were shuffling bands of old geezers who couldn't have moved away even if they'd wanted to.

You could hardly expect a seventeen-year-old kid who'd learned about Led Zeppelin and Jean Genet and doggy style to be happy about being stuck in a town like that.

I, however, was so bubbly and so eager to put on my goody-goody act for the teachers who came to check up on me that more than once my father shook his head and asked me where I'd learned to be such a cunning little bastard. I'd serve them a glass of cold barley tea and smile and chatter away—things that Adama, apparently, found it hard to do.

"They make me sick." I don't know how many times he told me this over the phone. All he did was get into arguments with his supervisors.

"They make me sick."

"Come on, man. Don't get so uptight."

"Ken, they all tell me you're really sorry about what we did. That true?"

"It's just a pose, man."

"A pose?"

"Yeah."

"What sort of pose is that? Huh? Where's your sense of shame? What would Che have said?"

"Look, man, take it easy, will you?"

"Ken, what about the festival?"

"We'll do it."

"You finish the script?"

"Almost."

"Hurry up and send it to me. I'll start getting the stuff we need together—whatever I can find up here, at least."

"What's that likely to be? Workshoes? I don't think we're gonna need any slag heaps, either."

Adama in confinement didn't appreciate jokes like this. He slammed the phone down. I called him right back and apologized.

"Hey, I'm sorry. Don't be so touchy, man. I'll finish the script soon and mail it to you, I promise. And listen, I was thinking about the opening—for the festival, I mean. Remember that girl we met at Boulevard? Mie Nagayama, the one from Junwa? We'll have her wearing a negligee and holding a candle in one hand, and the music'll be Bach, the Brandenburg Concerto no. 3, see, and she'll have an axe in her other hand, and up on the stage there'll be big plywood boards with pictures of Northern High teachers and the prime minister and Lyndon Johnson, and she'll start hacking away at them with her axe. Pretty cool, eh?"

This restored Adama's spirits a little. The festival was the only thing that was keeping him going. I knew how he felt. With the barricade now behind us, we were all looking forward to the next celebration.

CHEAP THRILLS

Matsunaga, the teacher in charge of our class, was one of the skinniest people I've ever known, having had TB for years when he was young. He was a mild-mannered guy, the type who'd probably never raised his voice in his life.

Throughout summer vacation he came to my house at least every other day. Being a quiet sort of person, though, he never said much other than "How's it going?" or "You're not letting this get to you, I hope." He also looked in on Adama just as often. Adama, apparently, would snarl at him, accusing all teachers of being stooges or capitalist lackeys, but Matsunaga would just nod and smile wryly and comment on the sunflowers in the garden or whatever, and then, after a while, he'd leave.

His visits came on top of a full day of giving supplementary lessons at school, and involved taking a bus to my place, then going on later to Adama's mining town. I could see the bus stop from my bedroom window. After getting off the bus, you had to walk up a narrow lane and a long flight of stone steps. I used to watch Matsunaga huff and puff his way up the slope, stopping any number of times to rest—a teacher with a history of lung problems trudging uphill to arrive at my house dripping with sweat, not to lecture me or anything but just to ask how it was going.... I soon found it hard to hate him.

"You may not understand this yet, Yazaki, but I'll tell you anyway. When I was in teachers' college I had six major operations—my chest is a mass of ugly scars. I even had fainting spells and so on. It was frightening, but, you know, people can get used to anything. I actually got used to the operations and the anesthesia and the blackouts, and I started to think, oh well, nothing really matters that much. In summer, for example, there are sunflowers and cannas and other things in bloom, and all I have to do is look at them to feel that way—that nothing really matters much."

Matsunaga used to say things like this from time to time. I'd stopped putting him down and had even begun to respect him, to think he was a hell of a teacher, in fact, but Adama and I were both a long way from "nothing really matters."

Adama was growing surlier each day, and by the time the second semester started, I too was getting pretty restless. The streets of a provincial city are empty of kids and grown-up men on weekday mornings; there's no one around but housewives and pensioners and infants and dogs. I remembered how unfamiliar the town had seemed whenever I came home early from elementary school. The smell of cut flowers would drift from under the half-raised shutter of the florist's; the owner of the shoe store would be just opening up for the day, dusting his shelves and yawning; the sounds of TV shows I'd never seen would murmur out of open windows; nursery school children would be dancing in a circle behind a wire fence, and old men would be crouched in the shade of trees, laughing together. The town was like a stranger to me then.

This was the town I was confined to now that summer vacation had ended. I began to worry about my attendance figures, because I'd ditched a lot of classes even before my suspension. Just to think about being **held back a year** was enough to make me shudder. There was no way I could take another year at that school.

One day when it was too rainy to take the dog for a walk and I was sitting at home playing the drums, the doorbell rang. Standing on the front step was Adama's mother.

"Do you remember me, Ken? I wonder if I could have a word with you."

She sounded pretty miserable.

"Please don't tell Tadashi about this, though. He'd be angry."

I was surprised to find that there wasn't a trace of Adama's accent in her voice.

"I know coming here won't solve anything, but I don't have anyone else to discuss it with. I suppose you know that the mines in our town are on the verge of closing? Well, these are difficult times for my husband, and he's just too busy right now to concern himself with Tadashi's problems."

She stiffened slightly and pressed a white handkerchief to her neck and forehead. *Oh, no*, I thought. *What if she starts crying on me?*

"I haven't talked to him for two or three days," I said. "Is he doing all right?"

Adama's mother gave a heavy sigh and shook her head. She didn't say anything for a while. *Don't tell me he's gone*

115

insane, I thought, and the thought terrified me. It was always the cool, calm, and collected types like Adama who tended to suddenly crack under pressure. *Don't tell me he's tying ribbons in his hair, wearing a flower-print yukata, and sitting at the organ, drooling and playing "My Little Butterfly"....*

"To be honest, I've never seen Tadashi like this before."

So it was true.... *I bet he sits outside at night howling at the moon rising over the slag heaps.*

"Of all our children, Tadashi is the most like me. He was always such a good boy, so well-behaved. If anything, I sometimes worried if he wasn't a bit too ... *placid* for a child. He never got emotional about things."

I thought about telling her she was wrong there, that I'd seen him almost in tears after watching the boxing cartoon "Joe Tomorrow," and snorting and gulping as he flipped through girlie magazines, but I decided not to.

"And now he gets so worked up, so rude to his teachers.... He's become more and more distant, even with me."

I considered telling her that it would be even stranger for a high school senior to be still clinging to his mother's apron strings, but I didn't. Her eyes were filling with tears.

"Before he was confined to the house, he used to talk about you often, about his friend Ken. I ... That's why I thought I'd like to talk with you a bit. What do you think about all this?"

"All what?"

"Well, college entrance exams, for example."

"What do I think of college entrance exams? Not much. Education in Japan today is designed not just to turn out useful members of society, but to sort people out and classify them as tools of the capitalist nation-state...."

I went on and on, discussing everything from the Joint Campus Action movement, Marxism, the lessons of the 1960 Security Treaty fracas, Camus's absurdist novels, suicide and free sex, Naziism, Stalin, the emperor system and religion, the mobilization of students, the Beatles, and nihilism ... down to the degenerate apathy of the old man who ran the local barbershop.

"I'm afraid I don't really understand most of that...."

I could hardly say "Of course you don't; I don't really understand it either," so I told her that the generation gap was no one's fault and nothing to be ashamed of. I hadn't talked so much in a long time, and it made my throat dry. It was no fun talking to Matsunaga—all you got for your efforts was a wry smile—and it was too embarrassing trying to talk to my parents about things like this because we used the local dialect. Try discussing, for example, Camus's *The Plague* in dialect and it would come out sounding something like: "*Da Plague*, see, it don' be jus' 'bout some disease. Be a metaphor, be a symbol for Fascism, **Communism**, stuff like dat." Anybody could tell immediately that you were just mouthing someone else's ideas. Chatting with your friend's mother, though, was a breeze. She'd never changed your diapers, or slapped you and made you cry after you'd fought with your little sister over a sweet roll, or worn herself out carrying you around strapped to her back. You could say the first thing that came into your head and convince yourself it sounded intelligent.

"But I do understand to some extent. During the war I did clerical work for an antiaircraft battalion, and I saw soldiers being killed in air raids. You and Tadashi, you're trying

117

to make a world where things like that don't happen, aren't you?"

I wasn't about to tell her that, no, I was only trying to draw attention to myself and attract girls.

"Actually, I think Tadashi's beginning to calm down a bit. Friends come to see him sometimes now, and... Oh, well, I know it's not really allowed, but Mr. Matsunaga has been kind enough to overlook it once or twice. Just yesterday two very nice girls dropped by on their way home from the beach."

"Eh?" I raised my head and gaped at her. "Girls? You mean from our school?"

"Yes. They're in a different class, though, I believe. A very sweet girl named Matsui-san, and another called Sato-san, I think, tall and rather attractive...."

Blood rushed to my head, and I didn't hear the rest. Lady Jane and Ann-Margret had been to Adama's house. Why would two refined, intelligent, courageous, and beautiful women go visit a guy who spoke a dialect you needed an interpreter to understand? And how could any "Lady" be so fickle as to deceive and abandon the knight-in-shining-armor who'd presented her with a copy of *Cheap Thrills*? On their way home from the beach, did she say? Don't tell me they were in their bathing suits? No, surely not, but still ... Lady Jane, with white strap-lines decorating her shoulders, fragrant with suntan lotion, goes way way way way way out in the boondocks, where there's nothing but slag heaps, to eat watermelon pulled fresh from some farmer's patch and cooled in a nearby mountain stream. And me? I get to console Adama's mother. Air raids? So what? You want to talk about real injustice? When Meursault shot the Arab, he blamed it all on the sun. I felt like Camus.

Life is absurd.

I telephoned Adama, still burning with rage.

"Hey, Ken," he said. "My mother went to your house today, right?" What the hell. He knew all about it. "Sorry. She still there?"

"Just left."

"Your parents there?"

"They're both teaching."

"Oh, that's right. So you were alone together?"

"I was the perfect host. Gave her a baumkuchen and a glass of barley tea."

"Listen, you didn't, ah … you didn't…"

"What?"

"You didn't try to kiss her, did you?"

"Don't be a jerk."

"Hey, just kidding. No, see, when she asked me for your address today, I figured she was going to your place. So she really went, eh? What'd she have to say?"

I didn't answer. I was pissed off, and I had my pride to maintain. How was I supposed to bring up the Lady Jane problem? A man who's been deceived by the one he loves is at a big disadvantage.

"What did you talk about? Don't tell me you sat there badmouthing me together."

"No, the truth is… Listen, Adama, don't let this get you down."

"Huh?"

"Don't go into shock on me."

"What do you mean?"

"Nah, never mind. I can't bring myself to tell you anyway."

"What? Let's hear it."

"I'd cut out my tongue before I'd tell you."

"It's about me?"

"Of course it's about you."

"C'mon, man, tell me. Please?"

"Promise you won't freak?"

"Spit it out."

"Well, it seems your mother talked it over with your father, and they're thinking about pulling you out of school and putting you to work. You've got relatives in Okayama, right?"

"Yeah."

"Apparently they want you to work in an orchard up there. By next week you'll be up to your neck in peaches."

"What's the matter, man? You're losing your touch."

"Oh, yeah?"

"Being a brilliant liar was about the only thing you had going for you, too."

"Thanks a lot."

"**Just kidding**. Oh, by the way…" Adama chortled. Cool-headed people don't do much chortling, and when they do it's not a pretty sound. "Matsui and Sato came to see me yesterday."

"What!" I said, feigning surprise.

"They said they were on their way home from swimming at Utanoura."

Utanoura was a beach just down the road from Adama's house.

"Is that right?" I sounded aloof, indifferent.

"I tell you, though, man, I'm not used to getting things like this from chicks. I don't really like it, you know?"

"What're you talking about?"

"This letter I got. It's just not my kind of thing."

"Letter? A **love letter**?"

"Well…"

"A love letter?"

"Well, I guess you'd call it that. It's in this kind of old-fashioned language. You know, 'To express my admiration and respect,' and all that. It's not for me, man. Give me Rimbaud any day."

The world went dark before my eyes.

"Oh, yeah, and Matsui asked me to give her your address, so I did. You don't mind, right?"

"I couldn't care less about Matsui. Chicks like that, I tell you, man, they got no brains, no culture, no sense of gratitude…."

"You serious?"

"Sure, man, I mean, what kind of a broad is that? I give her a copy of *Cheap Thrills* and she doesn't even send me a thank-you note. Look at my father—he writes to thank people every single time he gets a present."

"Present? That was Ezaki's record."

"To hell with her, anyway."

"I like Matsui, man, she's got class. I bet you wouldn't catch her writing this old-fashioned crap, like Sato."

"What?"

"Sato's got big knockers, but Matsui's a lot smarter."

"Adama. The love letter was from Sato?"

"Yeah."

A light came on in my brain. Ten thousand watts.

"Matsui's not human, man, she's an angel, she's in human form but she's an angel sent to me by God."

After expressing an inability to figure out how my brain worked, Adama told me to hurry up and finish the script, then hung up.

That evening, a **bouquet of roses** was delivered to my house.

"Aren't they pretty!" my sister said, clapping her hands. "They're for *you*, Ken? It's like in the movies!" I held her hand and we skipped around the room together singing "Mary Had a Little Lamb."

There was a note attached to the bouquet: "Hoping these seven red roses will take your mind off your troubles, if only for a while…. Jane."

My sister arranged the flowers in a glass vase for me. I put them on my desk and gazed at them all night long. Camus was wrong.

Life wasn't absurd.

It was rose-colored.

I finished the film script in two days. The title was *Etude for a Baby Doll and a High School Boy*. Long titles were popular back then. I stayed up till dawn writing it.

My father once told me about something that happened when I was three, at a swimming pool he took me to. I'd nearly drowned in the sea once before, so I was afraid of water and wouldn't go in. He tried yelling at me, coaxing me, prodding me with a stick, and bribing me with ice cream, but I just kept screaming and crying. Then a cute little girl about my age appeared. She called to me from the pool. I hesitated but finally jumped in—for her sake.

When I finished the script I took a short nap, then started right in on the text for the play. It took me three days to write it. The title was *Beyond the Blood-Red Sea of Negativity and Rebellion.* There were only two characters—a young divorcée and her younger brother, who'd failed to get into university.

"A play?" Adama said. "Who's going to act in it?"

"Me. Me and Lady Jane."

"Her I can understand. But you? Can you act?"

"Hey, I was the second of the Three Little Pigs in elementary school, man. I'll direct it, too, of course."

"You're not going to have nude scenes and stuff, like *Hair*, are you?"

"What do you think, you idiot?"

"But I bet you try to throw in a **kissing scene** or something. Better not, man. Matsui won't like it."

I crossed out the kissing scene as soon as we hung up.

One day shortly after the roses died and were carefully laid to rest in a drawer of my desk, Matsunaga showed up, smiling and saying "Good news!"

Our punishment was over.

After one hundred and nineteen days.

AMORE ROMANTICO

I sat at my desk in class for the first time in a hundred and nineteen days. The old school gate, the old courtyard, the old classroom—I wasn't the least bit happy to see any of them again. They had the same old air of cold indifference they'd had before my suspension.

Except for Matsunaga, all the teachers treated Adama and me as if we were bastard children they'd been stuck with after just one little slipup. We were neither heroes nor villains, merely inconvenient and unwelcome.

The class was English Grammar. The little gnome giving it was baring his gums as he read out sample sentences. His pronunciation was awful. It didn't sound like English at all; it was a language spoken and understood only in the teachers' rooms of high schools in provincial Japanese cities. I could imagine this guy in London—they'd think he was mumbling some inscrutable Oriental curse.

I noticed Adama looking in my direction. He looked bored. When he glanced away toward the window, I did the same. A group of elementary school kids was marching in pairs along the road outside. A field trip, probably. Beyond the steep hill in front of the school was a thickly wooded little mountain where there was a children's recreation area. They'd probably have a picnic and play Drop-the-Hanky or Who's-Got-the-Pickle. I envied them.

I remembered how, in elementary school, if I stayed at home with a cold for even three days, I used to miss my friends and the atmosphere of the classroom and everything. The reason I didn't feel the same way about this place after an absence of a hundred and nineteen days was that this was a factory, a sorting house. We were no different from dogs and pigs and cows: all of us—except, maybe, the baby pigs that got roasted whole in Chinese restaurants—were allowed to play when we were small, but then, just before reaching maturity, we were sorted and classified. Being a high school student was the first step toward becoming a **domestic animal**.

Between classes, Adama came over and sat on my desk.

"Narushima and Otaki were saying we should all get together."

"Get together and do what?"

He shrugged. "You going to pull out, Ken?"

"Pull out of what?"

"You know. Political action."

"You really think we can call it that?"

Adama laughed through his nose.

To me, there'd been more fun than function in what we'd done. You could say the same, in fact, about the fight against the *Enterprise*. Sure, some blood had been spilled, but blood was spilled at parties sometimes, too. Had they actually hoped to accomplish anything with their campaign? The roar of one Phantom jet was enough to drown out all the speeches and chanting. If they'd really wanted to break through at Sasebo Bridge, they should have thrown down their banners and placards and picked up rifles and bombs.

I was explaining this to Adama when I heard my name called in a soft, angelic voice.

Kazuko Matsui was standing in the doorway. As soon as I saw her face, my mind went blank. A hush fell over the room. The seven girl students looked up from their English dictionaries with jealous eyes, and the herd of male domestic animals averted theirs as if in the presence of something holy. Some of them even dropped their slide rules, fell to their knees, pressed their palms together and prayed. Not really, but I, for my part, was so flushed with pride my cheeks grew hot. I suppressed an urge to shout "Check it out—this is the woman who sent me a bouquet of roses!" and ran up to her.

"Um, I just thought I'd give you back your Janis Joplin," the angel said.

Next to her stood the busty nymph Ann-Margret, staring at Adama with fire in her eyes.

"It's good to have you back in school," the angel murmured. I felt like **Alain Delon** being greeted by a mistress on his release from jail.

"You could have given it back any time. There was no hurry."

From a corner of the classroom, Ezaki, the rightful owner of *Cheap Thrills*, howled "My record!" Lady Jane looked puzzled, and I made a mental note to kick the guy's ass later.

"That's Ezaki, grew up in a beauty parlor. His brain turned to mush from breathing hairspray. They say he's going to be put away soon."

She looked at me as if she wondered about my own sanity, then shook her head and laughed, a sound like the world's most beautiful bell—some relic of the Ottoman Empire, made of jade and purest gold.

"Listen, thanks for the roses," I said. "It's the first time that's ever happened to me."

"What?"

"I mean, nobody ever sent me any flowers before."

"Never mind, don't talk about it, it's embarrassing. It was the first time for me, too."

The first time.... She was a **virgin!** I was so stoked I asked her right then and there to appear in the film and the play. When the bell rang to start the next class, she mentioned the name of a coffee shop where we could talk about it after school, then hurried off. I walked up to Adama singing Gigliola Cinquetti's golden oldie, "Amore Romantico," and slapped him on the back.

"Don't go all goofy on me, man. What're we gonna tell Narushima and Otaki?"

"About what?"

"About what we were just talking about. You gonna tell them you think terrorism is the only way?"

"Terrorism? What're you talking about? Lady Jane was a virgin, man, it was the first time she ever sent roses to anybody."

"God, what a jerk."

Adama put on his famous I-give-up look.

During lunch hour, as I was on my way to the debating clubroom where Narushima and the others were waiting, I ran into the angel again. She had bad news.

"I'm sorry, but I can't meet you later after all. We have to practice for the opening ceremony of the National Athletic Meet."

National Athletic Meet. Was there anything uglier than the sound of those three words?

"Also, I heard that the boys have clean-up. You're supposed to clean the athletic grounds."

No one had the right to break up my date with her, least of all for reasons like those.

I walked into the clubroom shaking with rage.

"What do you think, Yazaki?" one of them was saying. "It's like, since the barricade, a lot of groups from universities all over the place have taken notice of us, and the Students Anti-Imperialist League at Nagasaki U. has officially offered to join us in a campaign against the graduation ceremony."

I was fed up. Absolutely fed up with it all. Was anyone there really serious about this stuff? I knew it was my fault that they'd landed in the shit—but who cared? If it weren't for the fact that they'd had a hand in getting me a bunch of roses, I would have told them to go fuck themselves and stormed out of there. Instead, I said:

"I'm pulling out. I'm going to be perfectly honest with you, so listen. Wooden poles, helmets, you're never going to get anywhere with crap like that, whether or not you join forces with Nagasaki U. or Kyushu U. or anybody else. I'm not saying I regret doing the barricade, because I don't, it was a good thing, but, look, I told you before, right? In a school like this you've got to use guerrilla tactics or you'll be crushed like flies. The same trick won't work twice. Anyway, what's the point of talking about disrupting the graduation ceremony when, after being suspended all that time, we can't even be sure we're going to be *in* the graduation ceremony?"

This prompted a long speech from Narushima, full of secondhand ideas about counterrevolutionary rituals and authoritarian governments and blah blah blah. He was in the middle of his spiel when the guidance counselor and two P.E. instructors poked their heads in through the doorway.

"What's going on here?"

The Politicos exchanged panicky looks, as if to say, *How the hell did they find out about this?* The idiots. It was only natural they'd find out. Our first day back in school, they were bound to be keeping an eye on us.

"You know you're not allowed to assemble like this," the counselor said in a low, raspy voice that cut through the room like a saw.

"But, sir, we're not assembling," I told him. "It's just that, since we were all suspended and this is our first day back, we thought we should get together and discuss where we went wrong, and how to go about being better students from now on, sort of like group therapy, isn't that right, guys?"

I said this with a big, sunny smile on my face, like an actor in the TV drama "Junior High Journal," but the others just stared at me blankly. Adama was the only one who put his hand over his mouth to hide a smile.

Our meeting broke up and I was taken to the teachers'

room, where I was made to kneel formally in front of the guidance counselor while about a dozen other teachers stood in a circle around me. Then they strung me up from the ceiling by my feet, dunked me in a barrel of water, whacked me across the face with a bamboo sword, pressed red-hot pokers against my back, and burned my thighs with blowtorches. No, but they did yell at me a lot and kick my legs with their slippered feet.

"Just because you're trash," I was told, "doesn't mean you can drag other students down with you. If there's something you don't like about Northern High, go on and change schools, the sooner the better. We met a group of alumni last week, and do you know what they told us? They all said they'd like to strangle you for dragging the name of Northern High in the mud."

The bell rang. I asked them to let me go back to my classroom.

"I'm paying tuition, I have a right to attend classes."

I said this without lowering my eyes, just as my father had told me to do. From the side, a hand flashed out and connected with my cheek. It belonged to the running coach, Kawasaki. I almost started crying, not because it hurt, but out of shame and rage at being slapped by a cretin like that. You couldn't let someone stronger than you see any tears, though; it made them think you were begging for mercy, even when you weren't. I blinked and took a deep breath.

And that's when it happened.

A chime sounded suddenly and an announcement came over the P.A. system.

"Attention all third-year students: assemble in the courtyard immediately. A rally will be held concerning today's opening ceremony practice and the cleaning of the athletic grounds. I repeat: attention all third-year students..."

Aihara and Kawasaki tried to dash out of the room to stop whoever was making the announcement, but Adama, Iwase, and a crowd of other students stood in the doorway, blocking their path.

Blue veins popped out on Kawasaki's forehead as he screamed at them:

"What is this? What the hell do you think you're doing?"

"Let Yazaki go," said Adama. "He didn't do anything wrong."

Behind him stood Shirokushi and his boys, my band, and various members of the rugby team, the track and field team, the basketball team, and the newspaper club, plus seven or eight fans of Adama's from our class. It had been probably one of the last group—someone with an anonymous-sounding voice—who'd made the announcement.

People were beginning to gather in the courtyard. Not all of the third-year students came, of course. You couldn't expect the gung-ho graffiti removers, for example, to join a spontaneous rally like that. Adama, in addition to being Mr. Cool, was a brilliant strategist, which accounted for the fact that Narushima and Otaki weren't among the group blocking the doorway. Those two were the dumbest of students, weren't any good at sports, and didn't stand out in any way, with the result that nobody gave a shit about them. Adama must have realized that if they were involved, he'd lose the support of the others. Shirokushi, on the other hand, as well as Nagase the rugby player, "Anthony Perkins" Tabara from the basketball team, and Fuku-chan, the bassist in our band, were all popular and had a wide range of fans. What's more, popular guys were used to leading the good life, so they were likely to have firm opinions about being forced into unpleasant tasks like cleaning the athletic grounds.

The courtyard was in a state of pandemonium. You could hear teachers bellowing at everyone to return to their classrooms. Three hundred or so students—about one-third of the senior class—were standing in the yard outside the teachers' room. When I saw Lady Jane among them I rose to my feet. My legs were numb from kneeling there, and I staggered at first, but resolutely steered my way toward my friends. The guidance counselor said something to me, but I didn't look back.

Adama greeted me with a handshake.

"Right on! Now for the rally," someone said, and we all shuffled off toward the courtyard.

"Ken, wait a minute." Adama grabbed my arm and whispered, "What do we do now?"

Apparently he hadn't thought this all the way through. Adama was great at making things happen, but there were definite limits to his imagination.

"You mean you haven't decided on anything?"

"No. I just figured if we got enough people together…"

"If I made a speech or something, I'd—"

"You'd be a **hero**."

"Don't be stupid—I'd be expelled. Listen, I'll go to the principal's office. You tell everybody I'm negotiating with him."

"And then what?"

"Just wait and stall everybody. I'll think of something. Oh, and tell Hisaura—you know, the student council guy—that I want to talk to him."

I went to the principal's office and knocked on the door.

"It's Yazaki. Can I come in? I'm alone."

Most of the kids had joined the rally just for the hell of it. If we kept them waiting too long, they'd get bored and end up doing as the teachers told them. I had to come up with some sort of results before that happened. Personally, I would just as soon have set fire to the whole place, but there wasn't anyone else insane enough to go along with that; and I had no desire to go through home confinement again or to be kicked out for good. I explained things to the principal.

"We'd like you to call off the rehearsal and the clean-up. If you do that, we'll disband the rally. I'll take responsibility for making everyone return to their classrooms. There's no telling what they might do otherwise. Not that it has anything to do with me, mind you—nobody's organizing this, it just sort of happened spontaneously."

The principal said he'd talk it over with the other teachers and told me to go back to my classroom.

When I walked out of his office I found Hisaura, the student council president, standing there.

"Listen, the principal just told me he's scrapping the rehearsal and the clean-up. Go tell everybody that. You want them to disperse, right?"

Only a jerk who was starving for attention would run for president of the student council at a college-prep high school. Hisaura was no exception. He was an ugly, useless dickhead who'd grown up on an orchard out in the boondocks near the sea. He swallowed my story in one gulp. The poor bastard didn't have a clue as to how to go about thinking for himself.

After scurrying off to get a bullhorn, Dickhead made the announcement exactly as I'd told him to. The kids in the courtyard let out a great cheer and began heading indoors, babbling about how groovy rallies were.

I didn't have my date with the angel, though, after all. The business of cleaning the athletic grounds was called off, but the other thing went ahead as scheduled, since it was a joint rehearsal with other schools.

All the same, it was clear that we'd achieved a victory. From that point on, the teachers stopped getting on my case. Even when I was late for school, or cut a class, or went home early, no one said a word. It was the same with Adama. They turned a blind eye on whatever we did, as long as it didn't involve other students. They seemed to have decided just to get us graduated and out of their hair as soon as possible.

Matsunaga was the only exception.

"Yazaki, you're a hopeless case," he once told me. "I don't see how you're going to survive out there in the real world." Then he added: "But something tells me you're the type who'll bounce right back no matter how many times you get pounded down."

"Iyaya" was the name I gave our festival production team. I took it from the "I" of Iwase, the "Ya" of Yazaki, and the "Ya" of Yamada. We decided the name for the event itself as well: the Morning Erection Festival.

Both my angel and the nymph Ann-Margret were eager to lend a hand.

And so a spell of rose-colored days began.

WES MONTGOMERY

With the help of Lady Jane and Ann-Margret, we were at last going to start making the film and rehearsing for the play; we'd get the Claudia Cardinale of Junwa High, Mie Nagayama, to appear in the festival opening wearing a negligee; and I'd sell tickets to the girls at Koka and Asahi, as well as to the radio tubes at Yamate High, boasting that this would be the first rock festival ever staged in Sasebo. The teachers ignored what was happening, but, piled on my desk at school every morning as the word spread, I found bouquets of flowers and stuffed animals and boxes of chocolates and girls' personal histories complete with photos and letters saying "I'm all yours, body and soul," and cash and checks and savings passbooks. Not quite, but it *is* true that I spent the entire day each day with an irrepressible smile on my face. Adama, however, whose sad destiny it was to have been born practical and realistic, tried to keep my free-soaring spirit anchored firmly to earth.

Adama, Iwase, and I were drinking café au lait at the coffee shop Boulevard, waiting for the two girls to appear.

"What the hell? This is just coffee-flavored milk."

Adama couldn't understand café au lait. I told him that

this was what **Rimbaud** had drunk when he was writing *A Season in Hell* and that anyone who didn't appreciate the taste wasn't qualified to discuss art.

"Rimbaud? Bullshit. Rimbaud drank absinthe when he wrote poetry."

"Who told you that?"

"It was in a book I read."

Adama was reading more and more all the time. Being a grind by nature, once he got interested in something he really delved into it. Not long before, it would have been easy to snow him on something like this, but it was getting a lot harder. He'd given me an earful, just the other day, about Bataille's *The Guilty Party*, *The Plague* by Camus, and Huysmans' *Against the Grain*, all of which he'd just finished. I'd acted surprised that it had taken him so long to get around to them, but privately I was a bit put out. It wasn't that I didn't read a lot myself, of course. *The Complete Sartre*; Proust's *Remembrance of Things Past*; Joyce's *Ulysses*; the *World Classics* and *Masterpieces of Oriental Literature* series published by Chuko Books; Kawade's *The World's Great Thinkers* and *Sacred Texts of the World*; the *Kama Sutra*; *Das Kapital*; *War and Peace*; *The Divine Comedy*; *The Sickness unto Death*; *The Collected Works of John Maynard Keynes*; *The Complete Lukács*; *The Complete Tanizaki* ... I knew the titles of all these books by heart. But the works I really loved and actually read and underlined in red ink were the great comic-book serials "Joe Tomorrow," "The Way of the Dragon," "Muyonosuke the Ronin," and **"The Genius Bakabon."**

Anyway, I was in no mood to let Adama's intellectual progress get me down. Today, after discussing our film and play with the angel and Ann-Margret, we were going to meet Mie Nagayama of Junwa at a jazz place to negotiate her appearance in the opening event. Nothing, and nobody, could wipe the smile off my face on a day like this.

"Ken, where we gonna hold the festival?"

Why did Adama always have to get so realistic about things? Didn't he have any imagination, any dreams? I felt sorry for him. No doubt it had to do with the environment he'd grown up in. I grew up surrounded by sunlit orange groves, cool mountain streams glinting with silvery fish, and ballrooms where American officers and their families waltzed the night away. Okay, that's a bit of an exaggeration; the neighborhood had four scraggly *mikan* trees, a muddy pond with goldfish in it, and a house full of whores who held marathon screaming matches with GIs, but at least there weren't any slag heaps. Slag heaps didn't have a speck of romance in them; they were symbols of the mad rush to rebuild the economy after the war. Slag heaps didn't inspire dreams.

"We need a hall of some sort," I said.

"No shit. What are you grinning about? You think you can make a festival happen by drinking coffee-flavored milk and grinning? What're we gonna do, rent the gym at Northern High?"

"They probably wouldn't let us."

"Of course not, you idiot."

"Hm. I guess we got a problem."

"You need permission if you want to use the Community Center and the Citizens Hall and all those places. You have to write a long description of what type of program you're going to put on, and the producer has to stamp it with his personal seal. You got a personal seal, Ken?"

"Shit. I hadn't thought of that."

"And what're you gonna do about the tickets?"

"Hand 'em out. Sell 'em."

"No, I mean where you gonna have 'em printed? If we go to some printer in town, they'll report it to the school."

He had a point. I wouldn't have thought it possible, but his slag heap realism had succeeded in wiping the smile off my face.

"You wanna print 'em by hand?"

"A thousand tickets?"

"Forget it. Can't have hand-printed tickets anyway."

To do it by hand or have them mimeographed was out of the question. We weren't talking about invitations to a birthday party or talent night at an old folks' home.

"So do we call off the festival?" Adama said. He seemed to be enjoying my discomfort. It was all he could do to keep a straight face.

"Listen," he said after a pregnant pause, "my brother's at Hiroshima University. I'll get him to have the tickets done at the campus print shop. They use real photosetting, not just typing or whatever, and since the print shop belongs to the university, it'll be about half price. As for the hall—you know the Workers Hall near the entrance to the base? They use that place for union meetings and stuff, so there's no real regulations or anything—all you need is a guarantor to put his seal on a form, and it doesn't matter who he is. The seats are removable, too, so if we have everybody sit on the floor, I figure we can get about eight hundred people in there. A thousand, no, but, hell, there isn't a hall in Sasebo that'll hold a thousand people. Even the Citizens Hall won't hold more than six hundred, and that's counting the balcony."

Adama was consulting his notebook as he reeled this off.

"The stage is about five meters deep—that's more than enough space for the drums and amps and everything, right? You got six lights on either side of the stage, and a projection room, too. I guess you don't need a projection room for an eight-millimeter film, but you need to make the place dark or you won't be able to see anything, right? Well, this place already has black curtains for all the windows. You can make it dark in about three minutes. Pitch dark, the way you want it. Oh, yeah, and the guarantor—I know this guy from the basketball team who graduated last year. He's pretty spaced out, and I already asked him to help. All we have to do is buy a ready-made seal and use his name and address, okay? Well? What do you think?"

"**You're a genius!** Café au lait is coffee-flavored milk! Slag heaps are the pride and glory of Japan!"

I pressed my palms together and bowed to him. He calmly told me to can the crap and to decide on the design for the tickets and get it to him by the following day.

"Yumi-chan and I were talking it over, and … Well, there are only two people in the play, right?"

The angelic Lady Jane said this between quiet sips of English tea, the drink of aristocrats. She was sitting next to me. Ann-Margret was next to Adama. She'd practically pushed Iwase off the sofa to claim that position, and Iwase had had to move to the next table. Now and again, the angel's thigh brushed against mine. Each time that happened, the sofa we were sitting on was transformed into an electric chair: a powerful current shot to the top of my skull, my hair stood on end, it was hard to breathe, my crotch tingled, my throat went dry, my palms grew sweaty, and the lonely expression on Iwase's face faded from my field of vision.

"Right. Just two people—a boy and his older sister."

Adama smiled knowingly. It was a smile that said my ulterior motive—to get tight with our leading lady by rehearsing alone with her—was transparently obvious.

"Well, see, I was thinking that Yumi-chan would be better for the job...."

I nearly dropped my glass.

"But I don't have half your talent," Ann-Margret told her. "I still think you should do it."

"We already decided this on the way over, didn't we? Yazaki-san, you know about the Performing Arts Festival last year, don't you? She won the judges' award for her Portia. And she was only a second-year student."

Ann-Margret covered her mouth and squirmed in her seat, saying, "Stop it, I'm getting embarrassed." She was leaning against Adama, her massive breasts jiggling beneath her blouse.

"Oh, yeah, I read about that!" Iwase said. "I think it was in the PTA newsletter. Ken, didn't we plan to do an article on Sato-san?"

I felt the sofa being transformed from an ecstasy chair into something more like a wet toilet seat. The words *Shut the fuck up, Iwase!* were on the tip of my tongue, but I figured they wouldn't win me any points, so I held them back and chewed on the rim of my glass. Adama had his head bowed and was laughing to himself.

"We can't use the drama clubroom, but I was thinking we

could rehearse in the church I go to," Portia the busty Christian said cheerfully, and I forced a smile, desperately trying to think of a way to insert a sexy bathtub scene into the script and to add another character—a girl the boy loved from the bottom of his heart. I quickly realized it was out of the question, though, and slumped down in my seat. It was out of the question because only five minutes earlier I'd been holding forth about how subtle, how revolutionary, and how pure and innocent the play was because it involved only two characters, and they were related by blood.

"Well, if you're sure you don't mind my doing it," Ann-Margret said, and I assured her in a feeble voice that nothing would please me more.

Sasebo Bridge had been the scene of the main battle in the campaign against the *Enterprise*. Spread out beyond it was the American navy base. The jazz club Four Beat, a favorite hangout of Iwase's and mine since our first year of high school, stood on a wide road lined with plane trees leading to the bridge. The club's interior had a particular smell we associated with black people. We called it the smell of the blues. It was in the counter, the sofa, the tables, the ashtrays. There had been nights when a sailor who was a dead ringer for Chet Baker and had a mermaid tattoo on his left shoulder played the trumpet, nights when black MPs took time out during their rounds to harmonize on "St. James Infirmary," and nights when hostesses from bars that catered to foreigners, their hair bleached brown or yellow or red, got into fights, filling the air with the smell of cheap perfume as they swung and clawed and kicked at each other. The owner, a man named Adachi, never gave us any flak even when we sat for hours over a single glass of Coke. Adachi was always stoned on booze or pills or dope, and whenever he got really loaded he'd start to cry. "Shit," he'd whimper through his tears, "why wasn't I born black?"

I thought it was the perfect place to meet Mie Nagayama. We'd told the angel and Ann-Margret that the next bit of business only concerned the production team. There wasn't exactly any need to lie to them, and the fact that I only did so to spare Jane's feelings is probably better left unsaid, because it's just another lie. Actually, it had been Adama's idea. He figured that if I were confronted with three beautiful women at the same time I'd lose it entirely and scare them all off by saying something utterly insane.

"Here to meet somebody?" Adachi said from behind the counter. "Judging by how jumpy Ken is, it must be a woman."

Adama nodded.

"She's the number one star in Junwa High," I explained. Adachi gave a scornful little laugh and turned his eyes—permanently yellow and cloudy from all the stuff he took—to the poster of Charlie Mingus on the far wall. Adachi didn't have much interest in women. He once told me he'd done so much booze and pills and dope that he couldn't even get it up any more.

"Seriously, though, she's a real knockout," I said. "Which reminds me, what do you recommend for background music? Something light, you think, like Stan Getz or Herbie Mann?"

Adachi nodded. "I know just the thing. We got a new Wes Montgomery record in—got strings on it. Mood music, man."

"Great!" I said. "That's perfect." But I should have known better than to trust some weirdo who went around weeping and wailing about not being black. When Mie Nagayama appeared, decked out in a red satin blouse, tight black jeans, silver sandals, eighteen-karat gold earrings, and pink nail polish, Adachi grinned to himself and put on Coltrane's *Ascension*. John Tchicai and Marion Brown were making their alto saxes squeal like stuck pigs, and Mie Nagayama grimaced at the noise, her almond eyes reduced to dark inverted commas.

We all went back to Boulevard. Even as I sat there pitching the festival to Mie Nagayama, I was painting a little picture in my mind of that evil bastard Adachi going into withdrawal, falling down in the street with convulsions, and being run over by a truck.

"Whaddaya mean, a festival?" she said, holding a Hi-lite between pink fingernails and puckering orange-painted lips to expel a stream of smoke. At that moment, for the first time in my life, I realized that a woman's lips could have something that not even Rimbaud's poetry or Hendrix's guitar or Godard's editing techniques came near. *If only I could make lips like that mine to do with as I pleased*, I thought. A guy would eat coal if that's what it took to win such a prize. I explained festivals to Mie Nagayama with all the passion of a man willing to devour an entire slag heap.

"I can't act," she said, crushing the ice from her drink between her teeth.

"You don't need to know how to act," I told her. "You see, you've been chosen as a figurehead."

"A figurehead?"

"Right. It's like I said earlier. We're talking about a festival where a thousand of the most progressive high school students in Sasebo come together, without any help from their teachers or anyone else. We're doing it on our own. They have festivals in Tokyo and Osaka and Kyoto—all the big cities—but they're not organized only by people like us. I bet this has never been done even in New York or Paris. That's how amazing it is."

"Paris?"

"That's right. Not even high school kids in Paris can pull off something like this."

"I like Paris."

"So, anyway, it's only natural that we'd want the most beautiful girl in Sasebo to appear in the opening event of a festival this revolutionary, right?"

Mie Nagayama stared at me wide-eyed, so taken aback she forgot to blow the smoke out of her lungs.

"Me?"

"That's right."

"The most beautiful girl in Sasebo?"

"Right."

"Says who?"

"Says the Northern High student council. It was unanimous."

She stared at me and Adama and Iwase in turn, then burst out laughing. Her laughter was loud enough to drown out Schubert's *"Unfinished" Symphony*, which was booming over the speakers in Boulevard. She pointed at me and said, "What is this guy, nuts?"

Adama started laughing, too, and said "Exactly" three times, and then Iwase joined in as well. I was pissed off but had little choice but to laugh along with them. The *"Unfinished" Symphony* was over before they all settled down.

"You guys are a riot," Mie Nagayama said when she'd got her breath back. There were tears in her eyes from laughing so hard. "All right, I'll do it."

There'd been a change in the casting of the leading actress for my play, but at least the two finest specimens of talent and beauty in the English Drama Club had joined the festival staff; the foxy queen of the private Catholic girls' school, who had a massive following of Greaser fans, had consented to appear in the opening act; the spaced-out Northern High alumnus had, for a measly two free tickets, agreed to lend his name as guarantor for the use of the Workers Hall; and the tickets had been beautifully printed in the Liberal Arts department of Hiroshima University.

I never got tired of gazing at those tickets.

Date: November 23 (Labor Thanksgiving Day)
Time: 2:00 P.M.–9:00 P.M.
Place: Sasebo Workers Hall
Presented by IYAYA
Rock 'n' roll, independent film, drama, poetry readings,
happenings, surprises, excitement and thrills ... all at
THE MORNING ERECTION FESTIVAL

The words were printed in bold type over a picture of a girl putting on lipstick and a volcano erupting inside an erect penis. Admission was two hundred yen. Through members of Vajra, the newspaper club, the English Drama Club, most of the athletic teams, Shirokushi's gang of juvenile delinquents, and various rock bands, the tickets were distributed not only at Northern High but at all the schools in the area. Iyaya was raking it in every day. I felt as if I was at the center of the world.

But just as Rockefeller and Carnegie aroused the ill will of the poor, I was to become a target for gangs from other schools.

LED ZEPPELIN

Walking through the foreigners' bar district made your heart beat faster. You realized how indispensable places like this were to the world. The Black Rose was across from a park that was famous for the crowds of homosexuals that appeared there every evening. Black velvet curtains hung over the entrance to the bar, bringing perpetual night to the interior. Sometimes, when the sailors suddenly came ashore at an odd hour of the day, you could hear the bright chatter of hostesses inside it even before noon.

I led Adama in through the back door. The owner, naked from the waist up, sat in the kitchen playing liar's dice with a waiter whose bow tie dangled loose.

"Excuse us. We're with the band," I said as we passed through the room.

"You kids from Northern High?" The owner raised his head. He had a cherry-blossom tattoo on his shoulder—no color, just the outline of a single flower in black.

"Yes," I said. Adama was frowning. He wasn't comfortable in places like this.

"Still a teacher there named Sasayama?"

Sasayama was a P.E. instructor who'd been with the secret police during the war. He was over fifty and had lost some of his fire by now, but in his younger days he'd been known to crack students' skulls open with a wooden sword. My father was always saying that, what with the turmoil and the shortage of men after the war, all sorts of crazy bastards had become teachers; Sasayama was definitely one of them.

When I nodded, the owner said, "How's he doin'? Give him my regards, willya?" before dropping his dice in the cup and shaking it. *What a creep*, I muttered to myself, looking at the unfinished tattoo. A guy who didn't even have the balls to get it colored in was the lowest of the low. Maybe he'd had some sort of run-in with Sasayama—got his head cracked open, probably. I always thought about Japan losing the war, and how pathetic our so-called fighting spirit was, when I ran into people like this.

They had no pride.

We went into the bar. Adama scowled even more. The bar smelled of America, which seemed to turn him off. The real America didn't smell like that, of course, but the houses navy groupies lived in and the hair of half-American kids and the PX at the base did. It was the smell of greasy fat. I didn't mind it. To me it just smelled of nutrition.

Coelacanth was playing the Spencer Davis Group's "Gimme Some Lovin'" without a drummer. Fuku-chan, the bassist, was doing the vocals, while Keiji on guitar and Shirai on the organ had their eyes closed and were whipping their hair around and sticking out their tongues, imagining themselves as Mike Bloomfield and Al Kooper. Shirai only knew three chords. In those days that's all you needed to know to be a rock musician. They waved me over, and I got up on the stage. Adama, still scowling, sat down at the counter, where middle-aged hostesses dressed only in slips were slurping up bowls of noodles. Fuku-chan gestured at the drum set with his chin. He always made a mess of the lyrics when he sang. Whenever he forgot the words, he'd just keep repeating "Don'tcha know, don'tcha know, don'tcha know." In those days all it took to be a rock singer was the ability to shout "Don'tcha know."

There was one customer, a sailor still in his teens who only had to cry **"Lassie!"** to convince me that he was actually Little Timmy. He was drinking straight from a quart bottle of beer and was desperately trying to get his hand up the slit in the Chinese dress of the hostess next to him.

"Fruits okay? Fruits okay?" said the woman, who appeared to be at least in her early sixties, and Timmy, suspecting nothing, nodded cheerfully and said, "Sure." With this, a familiar scene began to unfold. A metal plate loaded with bits of pineapple, mandarin orange, and peach, fresh from the can and adorned with a recycled sprig of parsley, arrived; Timmy, shocked at the price, broke his beer bottle on the edge of the table; the owner came dashing out and called the MPs; and soon poor Timmy, his pockets empty, was being bundled into a jeep.

Throughout it all, Coelacanth continued playing and Fuku-chan continued singing "Don'tcha know, don'tcha know." When the song was finished, he said "Thank you, thank you," into the mike, though by then his audience of one was gone.

"Did you arrange things?" I asked him.

We planned to borrow the amps and mikes for the Morning Erection Festival from Black Rose. To that end, Coelacanth was performing at the bar all afternoon for the nominal fee of a bowl of noodles and a plate of pork dumplings each.

Fuku-chan shook his head. "I haven't talked to the owner yet."

The hostesses at the counter were teasing Adama.

"You're gorgeous."

"Have a beer. It's on me."

"You got a girlfriend?"

"Sure he does. A doll like him?"

"Do you make out with her?"

"You better wear a johnny or you'll end up with a kid."

"Aren't you hungry?"

"You can have half my noodles."

"Want me to order you some stew?"

To these women, who'd drifted here from towns near and far to bleach their hair and greet old age steeped in the smell of America, Adama must have looked as if a halo were hanging over his head. If he'd started a new religious cult, no doubt they'd have all become believers on the spot. But Adama, who was born and raised among stacks of good, honest coal, was incapable of understanding these rough diamonds who'd contributed so much behind the scenes to Japan's postwar economy. He was sitting there twitching as one wrinkled hand after another came to rest on his thigh.

I turned to a group of three hostesses.

"Look, I wonder if you could try asking the manager if he'd let us use his amps on November 23. It's a holiday anyway," I said. "Yamada here, we call him the Alain Delon of Northern High. If you help us out on this, I could lend him to you for two or three days."

"He looks more like Gary Cooper than Alain Delon."

"What do you mean, you'll lend him to us?"

"You mean we can take him out on dates and everything?"

"Maybe I'll introduce him to my daughter. If she had a nice-looking kid like this around, she'd probably drop that black GI she's hanging out with. She's already had five abortions. I'm worried about her health."

Adama didn't find this funny. In fact, he got so thoroughly pissed off that he jumped up and ran out of the place. I hurriedly asked Fuku-chan to take care of the amps thing and ran out after him.

"Can't trust you, man. You're so fucking selfish you can't think about anyone else. You're going to lend me to those hags? You go around talking shit like that, you think I'm not gonna get pissed off?"

I said I was sorry **thirteen times**, but Adama still wouldn't forgive me.

"You don't have to get so angry. It was just a joke."

"Joke, my ass. I got your number now, man. You'd do anything to get what you want."

"Yeah, but listen, Adama, maybe it's because there's people like me that the human race has progressed this far."

"Don't give me that bullshit."

He was right, it was bullshit. And Adama knew me too well to fall for it.

"Look. Those women sold their bodies to get through the bad times right after the war. They sacrificed themselves for us. For the twenty-first century."

"That's got nothin' to do with it."

Right again. It was completely beside the point.

"Iwase-san came to our classroom and asked us to give you this letter."

It was in church—the church Ann-Margret had suggested we use to rehearse the play in—that Kazuko Matsui, lovelier than the Virgin Mary who stood there smiling down on us, said this. The church was on a hill above the station; it was the one you always see in picture postcards of Sasebo. Ann-Margret had apparently been going there every Sunday since she was a little girl. Maybe that explained her enormous boobs. Our Ann-Margret's boobs were in no way inferior to the real Ann-Margret's: they were simply magnificent. I doubt if it was true, but a kid I knew whose family ran a cattle farm and who'd once managed to sneak a look during the girls' medical checkup claimed that Sato's tits were bigger that those of the cows on his farm. *Dear God, please give me big jugs*—maybe she'd said a little prayer like this every Sunday of her life.

In spite of the solemn atmosphere of the church, the rehearsals proceeded smoothly enough because the priest, Father Saburo, was keen on the dramatic arts. The only problem was that, having been in a theater group for six months after graduating, he insisted on interfering with the way I was directing the play. Ann-Margret, for example, acted as if she were doing Shakespeare, throwing her arms wide and declaiming at the top of her lungs, which I thought was overdone and unnatural; but he praised her for it. He also went so far as to try to meddle with the script.

It was then, when I left that baby boy

in the snow at the side of the road,
that I realized what's really important:
risking your life for the right to say no.
Only by laying your life on the line
can you create words
worth risking your life to create.

"What does it mean?" he said. "Don't you think that part about the baby is a bit strong? Can't we change it?"

What an asshole, I thought. How could it mean anything? All I'd done was take a bunch of lines from different novels and plays and string them together at random.

When I saw Lady Jane, though, my irritation vanished. From a seat where each Sunday devout Christians bowed their heads to God, Jane gazed intently at Ann-Margret and me going through our lines on the dais near the altar. She put her elbow on the bible-rack and rested her cheek on her hand. The light of the evening sun poured through the stained-glass windows and illuminated her profile; it was like an Impressionist painting. Just looking at her gave me a deep sense of well-being. It was the same sort of happiness I'd experienced when I was at elementary school and had just bought the latest issue of *Boys' Comics* and sat down in a pool of sunlight, licking a popsicle, to read the next installment of "The Winning Pitch."

I was thinking how perfect this would be if it weren't for the priest when I glanced at Adama, who was reading Iwase's letter. He looked depressed.

> *Dear Ken-san and Adama,*
> *I'm pulling out of Iyaya. I'm sorry. It's been fun and exciting preparing for the festival with both of*

*you, but I want to do my own thing, and I can't do
that as long as I'm doing Ken-san's thing. I know you
two can do amazing stuff together. My thing may not
be much, but at least it's mine and I want to do it.*

That's what the letter said.

Iwase's house was on the bank of the Sasebo River, way
upstream in a neighborhood full of motels that catered to
lovers looking for privacy. The front of the house was a
shop where they sold buttons and thread, as well as stationery and even some cosmetics. Through the entrance I
could see a woman dusting the shelves. Iwase's mother, presumably. It was a tranquil scene; a shop exactly like a million others.

As we walked around toward the back, I found myself
thinking about the power of culture.

"Hey, Adama, culture's sort of an awesome thing, don't
you think?"

"Why?"

"Look at Iwase. If all this foreign culture had never come
to Japan, he'd be a plain old button seller all his life—he
wouldn't know about Led Zep or Verlaine or tomato juice or
anything. It's sort of scary, isn't it?"

"Well, hell, you could say the same about me and you.
You're just the son of a plain old schoolteacher, right?"

"Wrong. I'm **the son of an artist**. I didn't crawl
out of some co—"

I was going to say "some coal mine," but I decided not
to. Adama still hadn't quite got over the hostess incident.

There was a little garden in the back with cosmos in

bloom. Laundry was hanging out to dry there. Iwase had four sisters, so it was mostly petticoats and panties and slips, with only a few pairs of men's shorts. The flowers nodded in the wind, and from the window of Iwase's room came the sound of someone playing the guitar and singing.

> *Shining in a puddle*
> *is a sky deep blue*
> *Walking past together*
> *it's only me and you*
> *and it's always winter*
> *always winter....*

"What the hell is that? What's he doing, chanting sutras? Don't tell me he's joined Nichiren?"

Adama got pissed off again and told me to cut the crap. He said we were here to convince Iwase to stay on the production team, dammit. The problem with people from coal-mining towns is that they're just too serious about everything. Maybe it has to do with all the explosions and cave-ins and what not.

Adama tapped lightly on the window. Iwase stuck his head out and smiled his embarrassed smile.

He was a lot more cheerful than we'd expected. He said he was prepared to be in the movie and help sell tickets and set up the equipment in the hall, but he didn't want his name connected with the production.

"It's not your fault," he told us. "I'm not blaming you guys."

Adama, though, had taken Iwase's letter to heart. He thought that maybe his joining up with us had caused a rift between Iwase and me. After that dreamy session in the church, we'd gone to Boulevard, and it was there that we'd decided to drop in on Iwase and try to persuade him to stick with Iyaya.

"But, Iwase, I don't get it," he said in his calm coal-miner's drawl. "You're gonna be in the movie, right? You say you've got nothing against me or Ken, right? So why you gonna quit?"

"Adama, you don't understand, it's ... it's just that I ... **I can't stand myself** any more."

Adama and I looked at each other. *I can't stand myself.* That was one line a seventeen-year-old must never, ever let himself say—unless he was trying to make it with some chick. There was no one who didn't feel like that from time to time. Any seventeen-year-old face in the crowd in a provincial city, with no money and no pussy, was bound to know that feeling. It was only natural, considering we were right on the verge of being sorted and classified into different categories of domestic animals. But certain phrases were taboo, and you cast a shadow on the rest of your life if you uttered them.

"Hanging around with you guys, I began to feel like even I was getting to be a bit smarter. It made me feel good, but I didn't really have anything to do with what was going on, right? I can't explain it very well, but here I am thinking I'm hot stuff and, I don't know, it just started to seem ridiculous, you know, I just couldn't stand it."

"Gotcha," I said. What Iwase was saying was correct, it made sense, but just because something's correct and makes sense doesn't mean it's going to make you feel good about yourself. I didn't want to hear any more.

"Oh, by the way, Ken-san, you're going to use Mie

Nagayama in the festival opening, right? Listen, I heard from a friend of mine at the industrial arts school that the head of the gang there who's in love with Nagayama, he's going around looking for you and telling everybody he's going to beat you half to death. Maybe you ought to change your mind about using her."

Iwase said this just as we were leaving. He also reminded us that the guy was the captain of the kendo team.

Adama and I hardly spoke as we walked back along the road beside the river. Iwase was a gloomy fucker. Gloomy people existed by sucking energy from everyone else, and that made them a drag to get involved with. They couldn't take a joke, either.

"Adama, don't let it get to you, man," I said, staring at the ground as we walked along. "Hey, look, you said you liked this bag one time, didn't you?" I held out my orange shoulder bag. It had my full name written on it, with KEN in big Roman letters. "I'll swap it for yours if you want."

Adama looked at me and shook his head. "I don't believe you, man," he said. He'd seen through my ploy. Whoever was carrying the bag would be the target when the kendo guy attacked.

Which is what happened, just as we reached the coffee shop Boulevard.

All of a sudden we were surrounded by six high school dudes carrying wooden swords.

APRIL
COME SHE WILL

Six dudes carrying wooden swords surrounded Adama and me. They all wore crumpled school caps that could have passed for old rags, and on each cap was the **industrial arts school** badge. The swords gleamed darkly, and looked good and hard. Adama was already as white as a sheet.

"You Yazaki from Northern?" the leader, a big, pimply-faced, Neanderthal type, asked me. I was sure the swords would come crashing down on my head at any moment. I nodded, and my legs started shaking like crazy. To stop the trembling, I breathed in deeply through my nose and tried to look calm. If I let them know how scared I was, it would only encourage them and make it that much harder to fend them off.

For a guy who'd grown up among coal miners, one of the roughest groups of people in Japan, Adama seemed a bit on the wimpy side. What sort of impresarios were we, I thought; why hadn't we seen to it that we had a bodyguard or two? Too late now, though.

I'd got into fights once in a while up through junior high, but they were only harmless punch-and-wrestle affairs. For me, wooden swords and chains and knives existed only in **comic books**.

"Well? You *are* Yazaki, aren't you?" Pimples said, adding a menacing growl to his voice.

"Yes, I am. Say, aren't you guys from the industrial arts high? I've been hoping we'd meet up. See, there's something I'd like to discuss with you. Why don't we step inside this coffee shop so we can talk?"

I spoke in a voice so loud that people passing on the street turned to look, and when I finished I moved toward the door of Boulevard. Pimples put his hand on my shoulder and stopped me.

"Hold it."

He glared down at me, thrusting out his chin and raising his eyebrows slightly. He was copying the heroes of the gangster movies that had been popular a decade earlier, films that you could still see in small provincial cities like ours.

"You wanted to talk something over, right?"

My legs were still trembling, but I said this in a quiet, controlled tone of voice. My father had once told me that if I ever found myself surrounded by yakuza, I should be polite but not start groveling. Long ago, when he was in his twenties, he'd used a baseball bat on the chairman of the PTA— who also happened to be a yakuza boss—and the gangster's goons had cornered him and held a knife to his throat. "If they'd stuck me with that thing, I'd have been dead," he told me. "You were still a baby, Ken-bo, and I didn't want to die and leave your mother to raise you on her own, so I apologized. But if you get too humble with those bastards, they'll be more than happy to kick the shit out of you. So, even while I was apologizing, I suggested in no uncertain terms that if they laid a finger on me, a schoolteacher, their boss's son wouldn't have a chance in hell of ever getting anywhere in life. I guess I was pretty lucky, too, but anyway I came out of it without a scratch...."

I walked into the dim interior of Boulevard and headed for the table farthest from the door. The wooden swords and the oversize school uniforms didn't go too well with the music—Sibelius's *Finlandia*.

Adama and I sat with our backs to the wall, and Pimples and his boys occupied two tables in a semicircle around us. They stood all their swords together against the wall.

We were at least temporarily out of danger of having our heads split open at any moment.

"Is coffee okay with everyone?" I said, looking at each of them. The balance of power had shifted, if only ever so slightly. One look at their uniforms, shiny with sweat stains and torn here and there, was enough to convince you that these were Hardboys of the old school. They didn't go to game centers or coffee shops, because they didn't have any money.

Not being used to this sort of place, they were ill at ease. I asked the waitress, whom I knew fairly well, for eight café royals.

"We've been meaning to talk to you guys about Nagayama-san because we were afraid you might somehow have got the wrong idea," I said.

Pimples and his boys looked at one another.

"You got something to say about her?" the big guy said.

"Well, no, it's just that we were thinking of having her appear in our festival, and, of course, we knew we'd have to discuss it with you first."

"Listen, don't fuck with me, man. Maybe we can't do anything right here, but once we get outside you'd better be ready. It's gonna cost you at least an arm."

My legs started trembling again. The threat sounded real enough coming from an old-style Hardboy like Pimples.

"You been selling party tickets," he said. He meant the tickets for the Morning Erection Festival.

"Yes."

"You don't see nothin' wrong with high school punks doin' somethin' like that?"

"Ah, but, see, we're not out to make money, it's just that we have a lot of expenses—renting the hall, and the amps and the film projector and things."

The café royals arrived. Resting on top of each cup was a spoon in which a brandy-soaked sugar cube burned with a pale blue flame. It was unlikely that anyone in Pimples' gang had ever seen anything like it before; their jaws dropped open and they stared at their cups like people in old Edo seeing an **elephant** for the first time. What was disheartening was that Adama displayed the same reaction. People from coal-mining towns just weren't any good at pulling off stunts like this. Unless we both sipped casually at our drinks as if we did this every day of our lives, the whole routine was a waste of time.

"Oh, by the way, these are called café royals. What you do is, first you lick the flame from the spoon, real fast, then you drink the coffee."

This was meant as a joke, of course, but the dumbest-looking of Pimples' boys actually went and licked the spoon. "Ow! Shit!" he said, throwing it aside and grabbing his glass of water.

"You tryin' to make a fool of us?"

Pimples reached for his sword. The café royal ploy had only made things worse.

"Listen. You bought Nagayama a **negligee**. Why?"

We'd already taken in some eighty thousand yen in ticket sales, so I'd invested seven thousand two hundred yen in a white negligee for Mie Nagayama to use on stage and Lady Jane to wear in the film. When I'd shown it to Mie, just a few days earlier, she'd been crazy about it and said she wanted to borrow it for two or three days so she could see how it felt to sleep in.

"Oh, that. It's just a stage costume."

"Don't give me that shit. You can see right through it."

"You mean you've seen it? Don't tell me you went and ripped it in half or something? That cost nearly eight thousand yen!"

Whoops! I thought as soon as I'd said this, but it was too late. Adama gave me a look that said: *You fuckup.* Pimples opened his slit eyes as wide as they'd go. He was very angry. I half expected him to stand up and brain me on the spot.

"No, no, don't get me wrong, it's not like she'll be naked underneath, she's going to put it on over her uniform. See, what we want to express here is the innocence of a young virgin and, at the same time, her longing for, well, for sex, and..."

Adama shook his head as if to say it was all over. Provoking Pimples with that chickenshit question about ripping up the negligee had made me lose my cool completely.

The gang stood up.

"Enjoy the coffee. Enjoy it now, because your mouth is gonna be too mangled for you to taste anything for a while. We'll be waitin' for you outside. Make it quick. You got to face the music sometime, man."

After they'd stepped outside, the waitress came over and asked if we wanted her to call the police. I almost told her yes, go ahead, but if the cops and the school found out about the Morning Erection Festival, there wouldn't be any festival, so I had to tell her not to bother.

Pimples and company must have thought we were going to call someone for help; there were soon more than a dozen of them outside.

At Adama's suggestion I telephoned Yuji Shirokushi.

"You've been too flashy about the way you're selling those tickets," the Greaser said. "I heard about dudes from Asahi and Southern and the commercial school, too, who wanted to call you down and teach you a lesson."

"Well, we got guys outside here right now waiting for us."

"How many?"

"It was only six at first, but now it's about fifteen or sixteen."

"They all on the kendo team?"

"They've all got wooden swords."

"Listen, Ken-yan, that team came in sixth in the All-Japan high school meet. And the captain took first place in the Kyushu finals his second year."

"So?"

"So even if I bring ten or twenty guys, we don't stand a chance."

"But, hell, I can't call the cops, either."

"You got any money?"

"Money?"

"You got twenty thousand on you?"

"Well, yeah, but it's all from ticket sales."

"I'll have a word with this yakuza guy I know. You stay where you are. I'll call him right now."

"Wait a minute, wait a minute. Shirokushi?"

"What?"

"Can you get a discount?"

"Listen, Ken-yan, they crack your head open, you'll never be able to study again. They crush your balls, you'll never have another hard-on."

Shirokushi called back in a few minutes to say it was all set up, and before long the yakuza arrived. He was half black and, by coincidence, had once been a student of my father's. He brought Pimples into Boulevard with him. We reached an understanding over a glass of soda water, and Pimples retreated. He looked back at me as he left, the hatred in his eyes tempered by sheer astonishment that I knew anyone like this.

The yakuza snatched up the twenty thousand yen with his **pinkyless right hand**, then asked me how my father was doing.

"He used to slap me around a lot, but he was a good teacher. I remember once I did a picture of a church, and he said it was really good. Your father plays pinball, doesn't he?"

"Every once in a while, I guess."

"Tell him to come to the Palace Pinball Parlor. I'll make sure he wins."

He said he didn't think I'd be having any more problems of this sort, but that if I did I could call him any time. Then he shuffled off in his sandals, his black sports coat hanging loose over his shoulders and flapping in the breeze.

We began filming *Etude for a Baby Doll and a High School Boy*—an extravaganza on standard eight-millimeter film, part color and part black and white.

The first day, we filmed Iwase's face from the nose down and Lady Jane walking down a long corridor in the negligee. There was no story. It was a surrealistic treatment of the daily life of a student in a boys' high school who couldn't feel love for anyone except a milk-drinking baby doll.

Iwase played the student, a born loser who finds the doll lying naked in front of his grandfather's grave. He falls in love with it, and the doll stimulates certain dreams in his mind. Lady Jane appeared in the dream sequences.

The Bell & Howell we'd borrowed from Masutabe made a satisfying whir as it rolled. Unfortunately, I got the exposure wrong, and the first and second reels came out blank, but it was still great fun making a movie of our own.

Partly because of the twenty thousand yen I'd paid in protection money, we had to give up on having Lady Jane ride a white horse across a meadow in the highlands. Adama kept pushing for the big white dog, but I was dead against it, and in the end we settled for a white goat that lived near his place. So one day we all boarded a bus and headed out there to film on location.

"I made some lunch for us," the angel said, holding up a basket that smelled of sweet egg rolls. I sat there wishing I

166

could eat lunch alone with her. The conductor on the bus, a man with a hideous face, eyed us sourly as we played a silly little game called "Gorilla Boogers." To any question anyone asked you—"What's your name?" "What's your favorite food?" "What's your house made of?" "What's your hobby?"— you had to answer **"Gorilla boogers,"** and whoever laughed first lost. Lady Jane and Ann-Margret always cracked up at the first question, and Adama won hands down. "Gorilla boogers," he'd say, again and again, without ever seeming to find it the least bit funny.

Once we were past the suburbs, the bus rolled along beside a river, then headed up a mountain road. The autumn sunlight glistened in Lady Jane's hair, and the soft swells in Ann-Margret's blouse jiggled each time the bus swayed. The ugly and ignorant-looking conductor stared at us with loathing in his eyes as we laughed and shouted. That stare of his felt great. It seemed to me that we were just like the high school kids I'd seen in American movies of the fifties.

The goat was in a field beside a lazy river where pampas grass waved in the breeze. I set up the camera on a slope overlooking the field, intending to film Lady Jane walking along behind the goat, holding it by a rope, but the goat kept turning its ass to the camera and dropping **little balls of shit** or taking to its heels so suddenly that Lady Jane was jerked off her feet. Eventually the animal broke free, and Adama chased it for about five hundred meters.

We sat on the bank of the river to eat our picnic lunch. There were rice balls, pickles, egg rolls, fried chicken and cauliflower, and even pears for dessert. While the birds warbled and chirped in the trees, Iwase played the guitar and we all sang Simon and Garfunkel's "April Come She Will."

One day when the festival was only a week away, Lady Jane and I found an opportunity to be alone together. Coelacanth wanted to have a slide show behind them while they were playing, and I decided some photos of her would be just the thing.

We met at Boulevard and had a poignant cup of English tea, then headed for the American base. You couldn't go inside, but there were a lot of picturesque buildings near-by that I thought would make good backdrops: a cream-colored movie theater that looked like a Greek temple; the officers' quarters, with their ivy-covered walls; a Mickey Mouse clock tower; a church with its steeple painted pink and blue; a beautifully groomed baseball diamond; a cobble-stone street where people took their collies for walks; a road lined with plane trees whose fallen leaves danced in the wind; a row of red brick warehouses....

"Is the film finished?" said Lady Jane, smiling into the lens and sweeping her hair back with long, delicate fingers.

"All except the editing."

"Do I look funny?"

"No, you look great."

"Did you keep the part with the goat?"

"No, the goat's out. The image is all wrong."

She suggested we go to the beach when winter came.

"Winter? It'll be cold."

"I know. But I've never seen the sea in winter before."

I imagined us clinging to each other in the cold wind, and my heart began to pound.

Hours went by without my having any sense of time passing, and the next thing I knew the sky was the **pale purple** of sunset.

"I love this time of day," she said, her hands clasped behind her back as we headed home. I was taking care not to step on her shadow. "It's over so soon, and then it's night. But it's so pretty. I wonder if the way I feel will be like that—if it'll change all of a sudden."

"The way you feel?"

"Come on, don't be mean. I told you how I felt by sending you those roses."

I stopped and focused the camera. **"I,"** I said, and clicked the shutter. **"Love,"** I said, and clicked the shutter again. **"You,"** I said. Lady Jane smiled shyly. It was a smile to end all smiles, but it got lost in the gathering darkness and didn't show up in the prints.

VELVET UNDERGROUND

"Chickens?" Adama said, more loudly than he needed to. It was at lunchtime, four days before the Morning Erection Festival.

Almost all our preparations were complete. Thanks to Ann-Margret's over-the-top, weepy-voiced method acting and Father Saburo's meddling, *Beyond the Blood-Red Sea of Negativity and Rebellion* was a long way away from what I'd conceived it to be, but we were through rehearsing and ready to roll.

I'd finished editing the film, too, and we'd made arrangements to secure a projector and all the musical instruments and amps and speakers.

"Chickens?" he said again.

"Yeah. I'd like to get about twenty of 'em, but eight or so would do. You know any place we can buy them?"

"Butcher shop, I guess, but how we gonna eat eight whole chickens?" He must have thought I wanted them for a party afterward.

"You got it all wrong. I want live chickens."

"What the hell for? Don't tell me you're gonna wring their necks, rip 'em to pieces, and slurp up their blood on stage?"

I showed him a photograph I'd torn out of *Art Today*. It was a Velvet Underground concert in a ballroom in New York. On the ballroom floor were cows and pigs, glass cases full of mice, parrots on perches, a chimpanzee on a leash, and even a pair of tigers in a cage.

"Pretty cool, eh?"

"Tigers and monkeys and parrots—yeah, that's cool. But chickens? It'll look like an egg farm."

"That's where you're mistaken." As usual when I was playing the intellectual, I chose my words carefully. "The important thing is the spirit behind it. **Lou Reed** used birds and animals at this concert to suggest the chaos in the world today. The least we can do is make a gesture in the same direction."

Adama was well aware by now of my tendency to lift ideas from other people. He snorted and said:

"With chickens? You're going to suggest chaos in the world with chickens?"

But if Adama was anything, he was open-minded; he said he'd call a man he knew who had a poultry farm near Slag Heap Mountain. Adama was loyal—not to me, mind you. He was a believer, but it wasn't me he believed in. He believed in something that was part of the very air we breathed in the late sixties, and he was loyal to that something. It wouldn't be easy to explain what that something was.

Whatever it was, though, it made us free. It saved us from being bound to a single set of values.

We went to the farm that evening.

It was smack in the middle of a vast expanse of potato fields. The smell of chicken shit was overwhelming, and from

171

a distance the din of hundreds of hens clucking sounded like static on a radio.

"Whatcha gonna do with 'em?" said the man who ran the place as we walked around inside. He was a small, bald, middle-aged guy who looked exactly as you'd expect a chicken farmer to look.

"We're going to use them in a play."

"A play? What is it, a play about a poultry farmer?"

"No, it's by Shakespeare. And there's just no way to stage it without chickens."

The farmer didn't know who Shakespeare was. In a dark corner at the far end of the shed, about twenty listless chickens sat bunched together, hanging their heads despondently. The man started snatching them up and stuffing them into feed sacks—two chickens to a sack. The birds made a brief show of resistance, flapping their wings a few times, then gave up and went limp.

"Awfully relaxed chickens," Adama said.

"They're sick," the man told us.

"Sick?"

"Yeah. You can see there ain't much spark in 'em."

"It's … it's not some sort of disease that people can catch, is it?" I asked.

The man laughed. "Don't worry 'bout that. After your play you can wring their necks and eat 'em if you want. Nothin'll happen to you. What I mean by sick is … well, if they were people, I guess they'd be seein' a shrink."

He explained that there were always a few chickens that would suddenly go into a slump and stop feeding.

Adama and I stood waiting at the bus stop as the sun

sank toward the horizon, stretching our shadows a long way down the road. The chickens squirmed and rustled every now and again in the four sacks we were carrying.

"Adama, I know I said I wanted them as cheap as possible, but look at these birds. They're practically dead."

Hanging around with neurotic chickens was putting even us in a bit of a funk. Being with people—or birds or dogs or pigs, for that matter—who had no spark in them tended to lower a guy's spirits.

"Just listen to you. You didn't want to spend much 'cause you promised Matsui you'd take her out to eat **steak** after the festival."

"Huh? Who told you that?"

"Sato."

"Sato, right, that's right, I was going to invite you and Sato to go with us, of course."

"Bullshit. You were planning to use the ticket money to eat a steak dinner alone with Matsui."

"No, wait, you don't understand what—"

"Forget the excuses. We'll all eat together. Everybody."

"Everybody? Hey, steak's expensive, man."

"We can afford to go to Gekkin. I already made reservations."

Gekkin was a workingman's Chinese diner that was famous for its homemade meat dumplings. My dream burst like a bubble. I'd been counting on having steak and wine alone with the one I loved, and I'd already invited her to the fanciest restaurant in Sasebo. I planned to take her there after the show, when the sky was the lovely twilight color it had been the evening I took her picture. Lady Jane had smiled and bowed her head, which I'd assumed was a sign of consent. But then she'd gone and told Ann-Margret. I couldn't believe it. Jane! **How could you!**

"Listen, Ken…"

"What?"

"I know you've got a lot more brains and talent than most people, but…"

"Thanks. And look, I really did mean to ask you and Sato to come along with us."

"What about Iwase?"

"Oh, yeah, Iwase, too. He was in on it from the beginning, after all."

"And Fuku-chan? If it weren't for him we couldn't have got the amps and speakers, you know."

"Right, right."

"Then there's Shirokushi. Shirokushi sold ninety tickets, man, and look how he helped us get out of that mess with the industrial arts gang. And Masutabe lent us his camera. And Narushima and Otaki and Nakamura—they sold a lot of tickets, and they promised to help us set up the equipment."

"I really appreciate it, too. All those things."

"What do you mean, you appreciate it? If you want to thank them, the right thing to do is to feed them after the festival. Well, isn't that right? I know I might have expected something like this from you, but I'll tell you, when Sato told me about the steak dinner it really made me sad, man. Sure, the festival was your idea, but you couldn't have done it on your own."

I realized now how selfish I'd been, and it made me feel so rotten that my eyes filled with tears. Well, not exactly. The only thing in my eyes was a fading vision of a pure white tablecloth, a rosebud in a glass vase, sterling silverware, a sizzling filet mignon, a fragile crystal wineglass, and Lady Jane with a soft blush on her cheeks. And some real vintage wine—nothing like the Red Ball port I drank on the sly from time to time. I'd once read a passage in a novel that said that a fine, blood-red wine was "capable of stripping a woman of her reason." *Stripping a woman of her reason! Lady Jane stripped of her reason!...*

"What are you grinning about, you idiot? You're imagining yourself drinking wine with Matsui and giving her a big kiss or something, right?"

My heart stopped. Adama didn't have much imagination himself, but he was a genius at reading other people's minds.

"On the contrary. I was merely contemplating the shortcomings of my unworthy character." I said this with my eyebrows raised and my nose in the air, trying to be funny, but Adama didn't laugh.

Maybe it was because of having my dream of steak and wine destroyed that I now began to feel sentimental and sorry for myself as I gazed at the darkening sky. I wondered what the hell I was doing there at a bus stop on the outskirts of a dying mining town. I was also a bit worried that I'd used up all of Adama's patience with me.

"Hell, I guess it can't be helped," he muttered, more for his own benefit than mine, apparently. He stared at me. "You've got type O blood, right?"

I nodded.

"People with type O just don't seem to care much about anybody else. And you're a Pisces, right? Pisces is the most selfish sign. Oh, yeah, and you're the only son, too. A guy with that many strikes against him—hell, it can't be helped."

He'd missed one more: Pisces, type O, the only son, *and* Grandma's pet.

"A guy like you, if you stopped being self-centered, there wouldn't be anything left."

Adama looked down at the feed sacks squirming and rustling under his arms.

"Ken…"

"No, but really, man, I was going to invite you and—"

"Never mind that. I was going to say, do you remember how lonely those chickens looked?"

He was remembering the twenty birds huddled in a corner by themselves; broilers being forcefed in a cramped little shed. You might be a chicken or a human being, but show a little rebelliousness and the next thing you knew you were all on your own.

"When the festival's over, instead of selling them to a butcher or something, let's set 'em free somewhere out in the mountains," he said finally, still peering at the sacks.

On a beautiful, clear **Labor Thanksgiving Day**, nearly five hundred high school students flocked to the Workers Hall.

Otaki, Narushima, Masutabe, and the other members of what was once the Northern High JCA Committee stood at the entrance handing out "Smash the Graduation Ceremony!" leaflets and occasionally putting on helmets and making speeches. Yuji Shirokushi and his group of Greasers, their hair stiff with pomade, stood around in sports coats with their babes from Junwa and elsewhere, passing around half-pint bottles of cheap whiskey. The girls had turned up in all kinds of fashions; a lot of them wore their school uniforms, but you also saw painted fingernails and lipstick, tight dresses, pleated skirts, flower-print frocks, pink cardigans and jeans....

Iwase was selling mimeographed copies of a collection of his poems for ten yen apiece. He'd never let on to any of us that he was writing poetry. The gang from the industrial arts high showed up—to keep an eye on Mie Nagayama, no doubt—but without their swords. Being Hardboys, they got flustered and turned red when a girl from Yamate with a cigarette dangling between scarlet fingernails approached them and tried to strike up a conversation. Four black GIs asked if they could get in, and I let them through. Anything was allowed at festivals—except murder, maybe. The owner of Four Beat was there, and the waitress from Boulevard arrived with a bunch of flowers for Adama. The girls of the English Drama Club brought about a million balloons and filled the hall with them, and the half-black yakuza who'd smoothed out our problem with Pimples came dragging a pushcart and two partners in crime to sell bits of grilled food to the crowd.

Mie Nagayama walked on stage as the Brandenburg Concerto no. 3 boomed out over the P.A. system. Wearing the negligee over a bathing suit, she took an axe to some placards bearing pictures of the prime minister, Lyndon Johnson, and the main gate of Tokyo University. Coelacanth started their first set with Led Zeppelin's "Whole Lotta Love." Fuku-chan, as usual, sang "Don'tcha know, don'tcha know," again and again. Ann-Margret was the first to dance, making the great mounds in her blue T-shirt heave and quake. She was trying to loosen up for her part in the play. The black GIs whistled at her. Mie Nagayama started dancing, too, dressed now in her usual skintight black satin pants. I turned spot-lights on the two of them, and Mie's silver lamé blouse glit-tered and sparkled. As if drawn by that brilliance, more and more people joined in, and as the circle of dancers grew, the balloons began to burst. Coelacanth played three sets, in between which we staged the play and showed the film. Iwase grinned and blushed when a close-up of his face ap-peared on the screen. My yakuza friend came up to say he couldn't make head or tail of the movie, but he didn't walk out. No one left early, in fact. The angel was right beside me throughout it all. Coelacanth played "As Tears Go By" during their second set, and the angel and I stood face to face, gazing into each other's eyes and swaying to the music.

After a feast of meat dumplings, beer, and wild laughter, Amada fixed things so that Lady Jane and I could slip out for a walk by the river. In exchange for the candlelit dinner he'd deprived us of, he was offering an intimate stroll on an au-tumn evening.

The moon's reflection was shimmering on the water.

"It was all over so quickly," the angel said. "Do you think I looked okay?"

"In the film?"

"Yes. I looked funny, didn't I?"

"No…"

I wanted to say "You looked beautiful," but my throat had gone completely dry on me, and the words wouldn't come out. Beside the path along the river was a little park with a seesaw and swings. We sat side by side on the swings. The creaking sound they made seemed sexier to me than a Jimi Hendrix guitar solo.

"I always thought you reminded me of somebody," she said. "Today I figured out who it was."

"Who?"

"Chuya Nakahara."

My brain was in such a muddle that this didn't ring a bell at first. I couldn't remember any actors with that name, but then I'd never been told I looked like any actors anyway. Then it came to me: Chuya Nakahara was a poet. **A poet who died young.**

"Jane ..." My heart felt like it was going to burst, but I went ahead and said what I'd already decided to say. "Have you ever been kissed?"

She laughed. I was so embarrassed I turned red from my ears to my toenails. After a while she stopped and looked into my eyes and shook her head.

"Is that strange?" she said. "Does everybody do it?"

"I don't know." It was a dumb reply, but it was the best I could come up with.

"It's funny. I like love songs by Dylan and Donovan and people like that, but I've never even kissed anybody."

We both stopped swinging, and the angel closed her eyes. My heart was pounding, saying *Go on go on go on go on go on go on go on*. I got off my swing and stood in front of her. To say my knees were trembling would be a hopeless understatement; my entire body was shimmying like the moon on the river. It was hard to breathe. I wanted to run away. I crouched down and looked at **the angel's lips**. They seemed like a wondrous, separate living being, like nothing I'd ever seen before, a beautiful creature breathing pale pink in the dim light of the moon and the streetlamps, quivering faintly. I didn't have the courage to touch them.

"Jane," I whispered, and she opened her eyes. "Let's go to the beach this winter."

It was all I could do to say that much.

The angel smiled and nodded.

IT'S
A BEAUTIFUL DAY

Time drags a bit after a celebration like that.

My father once told me about taking me to my first Festival of the Souls dance, one summer when I was three. Apparently I was fascinated by the giant drum perched high atop its scaffolding, and toddled straight toward it through the ring of people dancing under the spell of that throbbing beat. He said it was seeing me standing there with shining eyes that first made him worry about me, wondering if I'd become the sort of person whose only goal in life is to find out where the next party is.

And he was right to worry. In 1969, when I was seventeen, it was the Morning Erection Festival, but even now, as a thirty-two-year-old writer, I always seem to be on the lookout for new excuses, and new ways, to celebrate. The rhythm of the drum that turned me on at three linked up with the jazz of the fifties and the rock of the sixties, and in one form or another it's led me all over the planet in search of bigger and better thrills.

What exactly that rhythm meant to me, I'm not sure, but I suspect it was just the promise of **endless fun**.

There's something empty and unreal about winter in

Sasebo, but I found myself looking forward to it, knowing that Lady Jane and I had made a promise to go to the beach together.

The day we decided on was Christmas Eve.

We met at the city bus terminal. I'd soft-soaped my mother into buying me a hooded McGregor coat for the occasion by massaging her shoulders for a couple of hours and saying things like: "College? Of course I'm going to college. I might even become a schoolteacher—after all, it's in my blood.... Come to think of it, Mom, maybe that's why you still look so young—because you teach little kids. You know what Yamada said to me the other day? He said, 'Ken, your mother looks just like Ingrid Bergman in *For Whom the Bell Tolls.*' "

The coat was a cream-colored, double-breasted affair with a fluffy orange lining, and the rest of my outfit—shoes, socks, pants, sweater—was equally preppy. Grinning at myself in the mirror, I applied a handful of my father's aftershave and imagined strolling through some little fishing village in this getup and saying, "Those fish there drying in the sun— they're flying fish, surely?" The locals were bound to think I came from Tokyo.

Lady Jane was waiting for me in a navy blue coat and lace-up boots, a basket dangling from her arm. As I walked through the crowded terminal toward those fawnlike eyes, giving a little boy who was singing "Jingle Bells" a pat on the head, I thought it seemed just like a scene from a movie. If everyone could feel as I felt at that moment, dressed in my **preppy** sweater and McGregor coat and about to set out on a little journey with my Bambi-eyed girlfriend on

Christmas Eve, all the conflicts in the world would vanish. Mellow smiles would rule the earth.

Our destination was Karatsu.

The bus was nearly empty. Apart from gifted, sensitive Simon-and-Garfunkel fans like ourselves, the only people likely to go to the beach on Christmas Eve were broke, defeated families who, unable to make it through New Year's, had decided to kill themselves.

Karatsu was known for its beautiful pine woods, its beach with somewhat bigger-than-average waves, and its pottery.

"You're going to college, aren't you?" I asked her.

"Yes. Well, I plan to."

"You decided where yet?"

"I applied to Tsuda and Tokyo Women's and Tonju."

I wasn't familiar with the stuff they printed in magazines about different universities, so I didn't know what "Tonju" stood for. From the name it sounded like a fun place, though, so I said maybe I'd apply there too.

"What?" The angel laughed. "Tonju is Tokyo Women's Junior College."

"I know, I'm just kidding," I said, turning crimson.

"Where *are* you going to go, though? Your class is all pre-med students, isn't it?"

"Ninety percent. But I don't stand a chance of getting into medical school."

"No? I think it would be great to be taken care of by a doctor like you."

I got all shook up wondering what she meant by this. Did it include the idea of me removing her blouse and feeling her chest, or having her lie on her back and spread her

183

legs?... The image was too rich for my blood that early in the day—we hadn't even got off the bus yet—so I summoned up a picture of Adama's face and had him tell me to get my mind out of the gutter. That helped cool me down.

The last stop on the bus route was in downtown Karatsu. The conductor told us they didn't go all the way to the beach in the off-season. I wondered if he wasn't just jealous and saying it out of spite.

It was quite a walk to the beach. I started calculating. It was now ten in the morning. We'd probably reach the sea by ten-thirty, which would leave us how much time at the beach? The angel's basket presumably contained our lunch, but even if we lingered over every luscious crumb of it, we'd still have hours to kill; we'd start to freeze sitting around in the cold wind with nothing to do, and end up deciding to head back early. What I wanted was a romantic **sunset**, the gentle melting sensation of a pale purple sky, when the very air around you is like a wine that strips a woman of her reason.

"You like movies?" I asked her.

At the entrance to the Karatsu shopping arcade was a movie theater. They were showing *In Cold Blood*. They should have called it *The Ruined Picnic*.

"Yes," the angel said.

"Look what they've got on. You've heard of it, haven't you?" Mr. Know-it-all. The fatal bluff.

"No."

"It's based on a book by a man named Truman Capote. It's one of the great masterpieces of our time."

And so, because I wanted to be on the beach at sunset, we ended up watching a film that definitely wasn't made for seventeen-year-old couples looking forward to their first kiss. It was a faithful portrait, in documentary style, of two men who lived miserable lives, massacred an entire family, and eventually died in the electric chair. The actors who played these characters had missing teeth; the film was in black and white; the strangulation scenes were more realistic than they needed to be and made even me look away once or twice; and the theater itself had torn, beat-up seats and smelled like a toilet.

In Cold Blood—the ultimate in gruesome true-crime stories—lasted a full two hours and forty minutes. The angel kept covering her eyes and whispering "Oh, no!" or "I can't believe it!" It wore her out.

I myself was so overwhelmed with fatigue and regret that I couldn't think of anything to say to her afterward.

"Shall we have our lunch now?" she said when we arrived at the windblown beach. From her basket she took some sandwiches wrapped in aluminum foil: cheese, ham, egg, and vegetable, with parsley on the side and little moist handtowels to use as napkins. There was fried chicken, too. The pieces of chicken had foil wound around them to make them easier to eat, and were tied with pink ribbons.

"Looks great!" I said in a hearty voice, but the shock of seeing *In Cold Blood* still remained, and I felt as if my mouth, my esophagus, and my stomach were lined with sandpaper. I stuffed my cheeks with a sandwich anyway.

There was a strong wind; far out at sea whitecaps were tossing to and fro, and from time to time the sand swirled up around us so that we had to cover our faces and close the picnic basket.

"That movie was something, wasn't it?" she said, pouring

me a cup of tea from the thermos.

"Pretty tiring, you mean?"

"Sort of, yes."

"Sorry."

"Why?"

"Making you watch a movie like that.... Some date, eh?"

"But it's a masterpiece, right?"

"Yeah. Well, that's what I read in a magazine, anyway."

"I wonder if we need things like that, though."

"Hm?"

"I wonder if we need masterpieces like that."

"What do you mean?"

"It's a true story, right?"

"Yeah, it actually happened."

"Why do they have to go and make a movie out of it, though? I already know..."

"Know what?"

"I know there's cruelty in the world ... Vietnam, and things like, well, the Nazi concentration camps, but I don't see why they have to make movies about them. What's the point?"

I had no answer for that, though I understood what she was saying. What answer could you possibly have for a pair of fawnlike eyes asking you why people had to go out of their way to see something ugly or depraved?

Kazuko Matsui was a gentle and beautiful girl raised in a loving environment. Maybe the world depicted in Capote's story *was* right next door, maybe it *was* necessary to take a good look at these things, but, in the end, what really mattered to her was, as she herself put it, "living life like the sound of Brian Jones's harpsichord."

186

We left the winter sea behind. We hadn't even eaten most of the sandwiches—let alone thought about having a kiss.

That's how 1969 ended for me.

Adama's a promoter in Fukuoka now. Coming from a coal-mining town out in the boondocks, he was bound to want a job that was as modern and Westernized as possible. After I took up writing as a career nine years ago and my first novel became a controversial best seller, he came to see me at a high-rise hotel in Akasaka where I was holed up working on my second book. It's not that way now, but at the time it felt pretty awkward seeing him again. Having suddenly become famous, I was under a good deal of pressure, and I couldn't help being wary about getting dragged back into the crazy sort of life we'd led before. We hardly had anything to say; Adama drank a cup of lukewarm coffee from a thermos I had in the room, and then left. Later, when I tried a cup myself, I felt like an absolute shit for having served such lousy coffee to a friend I'd spent my seventeenth year with.

Fuku-chan, the bassist and singer in Coelacanth, now lives in Fukuoka, too. He runs a record shop there, specializing in jazz, and also helps produce concerts occasionally. He always sends me a copy of any good new salsa or reggae record. Every time we meet, we sing Janis Joplin songs together, and when we forget the words it's still "Don'tcha know, don'tcha know."

It's been years since I heard from Otaki and Narushima, the leaders of the Northern High Joint Campus Action Committee, but when I first came to Tokyo, after taking the general exam and getting into a city college, I visited the boardinghouse they were living in. Scattered about in their room were helmets and wooden poles and leaflets, and a girl in a blouse and jeans and no makeup. We listened to some protest songs and had cups of instant noodles.

Yuji Shirokushi, the head Greaser, became a doctor. I met him once when he was still in medical school. He said that of all the bar girls and strippers he'd met at the joints he went to, only two so far had refused to spend the night with him after he'd shown them his med school I.D. card.

The nymph Yumi "Ann-Margret" Sato is happily married and still in Sasebo as far as I know.

When I first arrived in Tokyo I saw a lot of Iwase, but for the past several years I haven't been able to get in touch with him. Someone told me he was playing guitar and singing in a downtown strip joint, though I'm not sure if it's true. Back then he was living with a girl who wanted to be a painter, but the last time I saw him he said they'd split up.

Mie Nagayama became a beautician.

Sasaki, the detective who interrogated me, always sends me a New Year's card.
Happy New Year. There's nothing likable about the juvenile delinquents nowadays....

"Pimples," leader of the industrial arts gang, lost four fingers of his right hand in a hydraulic press while working at Sasebo Heavy Industries. He's given up kendo.

The half-black yakuza went straight and now runs a coffee shop in Sasebo. My autograph hangs in a frame on the wall there.

Kawasaki and Aihara, the P.E. instructors, took jobs at other schools and are no longer in Sasebo.

My homeroom teacher, Matsunaga, left Northern High to work at a girls' high school somewhere. Recently, he told me off in the same tone of voice he'd used when I was still a student.

"Yazaki, get a haircut. You look terrible."

The vice president of the student council—the guy who'd clung to my collar and cried the day after the barricade— joined the Red Army Faction while he was at Kyoto University, and was later arrested in Singapore.

Nakamura, of "doo-doo" fame, now works as a PR man in Nagasaki. I bumped into him once when I went there to give a lecture. He'd been reading the monthly installments of this novel in a magazine and told me, "I was always afraid you'd write about that business sometime, and now you've gone and done it, haven't you?" He looked pleased.

My love affair with the angel Kazuko "Lady Jane" Matsui came to an end on a rainy Sunday in February 1970, after she'd had **a change of heart**.

The angel had found herself an older boyfriend.

The boyfriend went to medical school at Kyushu University, while she was a student at Tonju. I continued seeing her occasionally—even though we were now **"just friends"**—up to the time she announced, in a park where the last petals on the cherry trees were falling, that she was going to marry him. That night I consumed an entire bottle of Suntory Kaku whiskey, half a bottle of Suntory White, a bottle of Red Ball port, two plates of curry and two bowls of beef stew; then, in the wee hours of the morning, I pulled out my flute and started playing it, as a result of which a young yakuza who lived in my apartment building informed me that I was disturbing his sleep and punched me four times in the face.

Since becoming a novelist, I've received several letters from her and one phone call. When she telephoned I was listening to Boz Scaggs's "We're All Alone."

"That's Boz Scaggs, isn't it?"

"Yes."

"Do you still listen to Paul Simon?"

"No, not any more."

"I suppose not. I still do, though, sometimes."

"How are you getting on?"

She didn't answer that one. A few days later she sent me a letter.

Hearing your voice, with Boz Scaggs in the background, made me feel I was back at school. I like Boz Scaggs, too, but I don't listen to him these days. My life has been just one lousy thing after another for the last twelve months, so I listen to Tom Waites a lot. I'm trying to forget about the bad stuff, but I guess the only way to do that is to start a new life....

At the end of the letter, typed in English, was a line from a Paul Simon song:

"Still crazy after all these years...."

The chickens that took part in the Morning Erection Festival were released by Adama in the mountains near his home after the mines had closed down. They were featured once in a local paper:

WILD SUPERCHICKENS
TEN METERS IN A SINGLE BOUND!